Ruth

The Final Farewell

Kevin Kirk Chronicles

a novel

Patricia Wiles

Covenant Communications, Inc.

Cover illustration by Jason Quinn.

Cover design by Jessica A. Warner © 2007 by Covenant Communications, Inc.

Published by Covenant Communications, Inc.
American Fork, Utah

Copyright © 2007 by Patricia Wiles

All rights reserved. No part of this book may be reproduced in any format or in any medium without the written permission of the publisher, Covenant Communications, Inc., P.O. Box 416, American Fork, UT 84003.

This is a work of fiction. The characters, names, incidents, places, and dialogue are products of the author's imagination, and are not to be construed as real.

Printed in Canada
First Printing: May 2007

13 12 11 10 09 08 07   10 9 8 7 6 5 4 3 2 1

ISBN 978-1-59811-353-2

This book is dedicated to
the good people living in the California Riverside Mission
of The Church of Jesus Christ of Latter-day Saints.
Thank you for supporting, encouraging, and caring for
my son while he labored in your corner of
the Lord's vineyard from 2005 to 2007.

Acknowledgments

I am grateful to Emily Halverson for her input—and to Angela Eschler for her patience—during the editing of this book.

And, as always, I am grateful for the love and support of my husband and my precious children.

Chapter One

It was late summer in Armadillo, Arkansas, and hotter than the Cow Palace restaurant's Great Balls of Fire Cow Pattie with double jalapeños. Dr. Alfred Leopold Wallace stood in front of the flower-covered archway, shifting his weight from one foot to the other.

I couldn't help but think that since it was like an oven outside, it was a perfect time for my old half-baked, eighth-grade life sciences teacher to marry someone as half-baked as himself—Cassiopeia, otherwise known as Gladys Penelope Melon. Cassiopeia was Melonhead's mother—Melonhead being one of my two best friends at the time. Melonhead liked to say his mother was a free spirit. Most people just thought she was weird.

Cassiopeia wore togas, ate tofu, and claimed she could feel people's auras. Yet I couldn't say she was weird for having her wedding at the Paramount Funeral Home. It was my parents' home and business, after all, and my mother and Cassiopeia were good friends in spite of their different personalities.

Besides, this wasn't the first wedding we'd had at the Paramount. Marcy and Marshall had said "I do" in our outdoor sitting area a few years before. Mom and Dad had hired Marcy as an apprentice during their first year at the Paramount. She was so affectionate, warm, and fun that my parents couldn't help but love her. Soon Marcy was calling my parents Momma and Daddy K. And Mom and Dad were telling people Marcy was their daughter—never mind the odd looks they got because they were white and Marcy was African-American. I didn't care what anyone else thought either. To me, Marcy was truly my sister.

When Marcy finally gave in to her boyfriend Marshall's proposals, she wanted to have her wedding at home—our funeral home. The setting, though it sounded creepy, was anything but. Mom had cultivated the sitting area outside into a major flower garden, almost like something you'd see in a magazine. There was a kidney-shaped fish pond with plenty of fat koi, antique iron benches to sit on, and a cool ancient-looking sundial Mom had picked up at the Memphis Mega Flea Market.

So when Cassiopeia announced her engagement to Dr. Wallace, Mom offered to host the ceremony. Like she said, if you ignored the hearse that was parked close by, the sitting area made a great spot for a wedding.

Dr. Wallace's high-pitched complaint interrupted my thoughts. "Is it time to commence with the ceremony?" He tugged at his bow tie and stretched his neck. His face was red—either from nerves or from the heat-absorbing black tuxedo. His white chrysanthemum boutonniere had withered to brown and now hung limp from his lapel.

I loosened my tie so the sweat could run freely past my collar. "Shouldn't be long. Marcy got the bouquet out of the refrigerator a minute ago."

My grandfather set up the last folding chair and wiped his brow. "Here's your first lesson in marriage, Doc. Women are never ready on time for anything."

There was a brief, merciful blast of cool air when Melonhead opened the French doors. "Mom's on her way." He trotted down the aisle and took his place as best man.

Mormons that meet in small congregations call their lay ministers branch presidents. Armadillo had as small a Mormon congregation as you could get. President Carter (not to be confused with the former president of the United States) was our branch president. He took his place under the arch. He held a Bible in one hand and a marriage license in the other. His wife herded their two young sons, Dylan and Derek, to a row of seats in the back. Their daughter Dani—my other best friend— mopped my forehead with a tissue.

"You're going to melt in that suit."

I nodded. "It's kinda warm."

She took a handheld, battery-operated fan from her bag, held it to my face, and turned it on. "How's that?"

I laughed. "Maybe it will dry the sweat on my lip."

"Dani!" Lily B, Marcy and Marshall's daughter, burst through the doors, releasing another blessed gust of air-conditioning. She ran to Dani with outstretched arms. "Dani hold me?"

"You betcha." Dani picked up Lily B and set her on her hip. "Who's my bestest three-year-old friend?"

Lily B's black eyes shone. She smoothed Dani's hair with her chubby brown hands. "Dani is my best friend of all."

"What about me?" I stuck my bottom lip out in a pout. "What about Uncle Kevin? I thought I was your best friend."

Lily B shook her head. "Silly Unka Kebin."

"Who told you I was silly?"

Lily B giggled. "Mommy."

Dani laughed. "I think *you're* silly." She poked Lily B's tummy. Lily B poked her back.

Marcy stuck her head out the doors. "The bride's on her way." She then stepped out and held the doors for Dad as he carried out the CD player and a stack of CDs.

"Gam-pa K!" Lily B shouted. She squirmed out of Dani's arms and ran to my father. "Gam-pa K, can I play wif it?"

Dad almost dropped the CDs when Lily B grabbed his leg. "No. It's time for the wedding, princess." Dad set the player and the discs on a small table behind the last row of chairs. "Where's your flower basket?"

Lily B clamped her hands over her mouth and ran back inside.

"She's so funny," Dani said. "Isn't she adorable in that flower girl outfit?"

"Yeah." I checked my watch. Cassiopeia was already ten minutes late.

"When I get married, I'm going to have five bridesmaids, and my flower girl is going to wear a pink taffeta dress and real roses in her hair. Pink ones."

"I didn't think you could have stuff like that in a temple wedding."

"You can't. That's why I'm having a real wedding ceremony first. I want to walk down the aisle and wear a beautiful dress with a long train covered in sequins. The church will be full of flowers, and there'll be a photographer taking pictures and everything."

Our church met in the old Fix-Rite Hardware store. It would look stupid to have a big wedding in there. I laughed. "If you're going to get married in our church building, make sure you don't trip as you walk through the talking doors that say 'Welcome to Fix-Rite.'"

Dani scowled at me. "I don't mean *our* church building. I'll rent the big Baptist church downtown—the one with the huge stained glass windows." Her eyes glazed over as she daydreamed. "We'll even decorate the outside. Pink and white silk bows on the doors, silk streamers twirled around the handrails—it'll be gorgeous."

"What about marrying in the temple?"

"I'll go to the temple—right after the big wedding. Like the next week, maybe after the honeymoon."

"Two weddings? That's dumb."

"Why can't I have the big wedding I want? Everybody else has them. If I go to the temple later, it shouldn't matter as long as I do it."

Mom peeked out the door. "We're ready!" She nodded to Melonhead and then to Dad, who was standing at attention next to the CD player.

Dani went to sit with her mom. After she sat down she smiled and waved at me. I smiled back.

I'd never heard Dani talk like that before, like going to the temple wasn't all that important. Most of the time, she was the one telling me that I wasn't taking church things seriously. I wondered what had made her change her mind.

Melonhead walked backwards from President Carter to the French doors, unrolling rice paper on top of the yellow carpet runner. Cassiopeia would tiptoe over it on her way to the makeshift altar.

The patio light flickered—the signal that Cassiopeia was ready.

Dad punched the ON button, and the bridal march began.

Honey, Melonhead's little sister, was the maid of honor. She wore a gauzy yellow dress and carried a bunch of wildflowers tied together with a thin yellow ribbon. The rice paper made soft crackling sounds with each step of her bare feet. Dr. Wallace gave her an awkward wave.

Lily B was next. When her feet touched the rice paper, she giggled.

"Go on," Marcy whispered. "Follow Honey."

The yellow ribbons on the ends of her dark braids flapped as she nodded. She took slow, careful steps, hamming it up for the crowd.

"The petals—drop your petals."

Lily B frowned at her mother. She didn't understand.

"In your basket, baby." Marshall leaned over Marcy's pregnant tummy and pointed to the yellow basket Lily B carried in her hand.

"Oh! Da petals!" Lily B reached in the basket and pulled out a handful.

Marcy nodded. "Good girl. Now drop them."

Lily B put the petals back in the basket and raised it over her head.

Marshall and Marcy were frantic. "No, Lily!"

"Petals!" Lily B squealed. She turned the basket over and was hit by a deluge of multi-colored rose petals. She threw the basket down and ran to Honey, ripping the rice paper with her tiny feet. "See my petals? Dey're on my head!"

Honey brushed the petals off Lily B's head. Murmurs of laughter flowed through the crowd.

The French doors opened and Cassiopeia emerged. She looked like some kind of elf princess in her bare feet and flowing white dress. She let her wavy brown hair float free instead of brushing it up into a bun like usual. An enormous wreath of wildflowers circled the top of her head, and she carried an even bigger bouquet of wildflowers in her arms.

As track one of the *Blissful Music for Blushing Brides* CD concluded, Cassiopeia took her place beside Dr. Wallace and handed the flowers to Honey.

President Carter cleared his throat. "We are here today to witness the marriage of Cassiopeia—I mean, Gladys Penelope Melon—to Alfred Leopold Wallace."

Dr. Wallace leaned toward President Carter. "*Doctor.* Don't forget the *Doctor.* I'm a Ph.D., you know."

President Carter dabbed at the sweat dripping from his temples. Then he raised his voice: "We are here today to witness the marriage of Gladys Penelope Melon to Dr. Alfred Leopold Wallace."

Dr. Wallace nodded his approval. Then Cassiopeia took Dr. Wallace's hand, and all at once his legs began to wobble.

The ceremony went on, the phrase *until death* being repeated more times than I cared to hear. I never gave it much thought until after my parents were sealed in the temple, and I had been sealed to them, during my junior year of high school. Since then, whenever I heard the until-death-do-us-part portion of a wedding, it made the whole ceremony seem pointless. I reminded myself, though, that this wedding wasn't pointless to Cassiopeia and Dr. Wallace. They just didn't have a testimony of eternal families yet. Would they ever?

Melonhead stood beside Dr. Wallace as his best man. His hands were behind his back, and I chuckled to myself when I noticed that his fingers were crossed.

I was going to miss Melonhead.

Soon the ceremony was over. "You may kiss the bride," President Carter said to the new Dr. and Mrs. Wallace.

Dr. Wallace pecked Cassiopeia on the cheek.

Everyone clapped and cheered, including Dani.

I frowned. If anyone here should have a testimony of eternal families, Dani should. Why was it more important to her to have a big wedding than to have her wedding in the right place?

Later, in the guest kitchen, I was sitting alone at one of the tables and eating a huge chunk of wedding cake when Dr. Wallace sat down beside me.

"So, Kevin Kirk, you are a senior. The time has come for you to consider colleges. Have you narrowed your selection?" Dr. Wallace shoved a big piece of cake in his mouth. A blob of yellow icing hung from his lip as he chewed.

I wiped my mouth with my napkin, hoping he'd get the hint. He didn't.

"I've thought about it."

"I assume you are still an excellent student?"

I nodded.

"Are you still interested in life science?"

"I'd like to major in biology."

Dr. Wallace finally wiped his mouth. But instead of getting rid of the icing, he just smeared it. "I've accepted a position at Nelson-Barrett University. They have one of the most prestigious research programs in the South," he said, sounding like he'd memorized the line from a recruiter's brochure.

"Congratulations." Of course I already knew he was going to teach there. Melonhead and I had been talking about it for weeks. I was happy for Dr. Wallace. I knew he liked teaching life sciences at Armadillo Middle, but his dream had always been to teach and do research at a real university. But I wished Melonhead didn't have to move with him.

"They are recruiting students for their new undergraduate research program. They are offering a limited number of full scholarships."

The pineapple punch was so sugary it made my teeth hurt. I popped a few salted peanuts into my mouth to counteract the sweetness.

"These students will assist the professors on various projects. I want to recommend you to the committee."

I choked on the peanuts. I grabbed another yellow cocktail napkin and coughed into it.

Dr. Wallace slapped me on the back with his bony hand. "Should I perform the Heimlich maneuver?"

I shook my head no and coughed some more.

Dr. Wallace handed me my punch cup. "Take another sip."

The syrupy punch slid down my throat. I almost gagged from the sweetness, but at least it made me stop coughing. "You would do that for me? Recommend me for a full scholarship?"

"Of course," Dr. Wallace said matter-of-factly. "Research is in your nature. You would be a credit to the school and to the program. Why wouldn't I consider you?"

I wanted to hug Dr. Wallace, but of course I didn't. "You bet I'd be interested."

Then—just as clear as Dr. Wallace's offer—I heard another voice: *What about a mission?* I looked around, but there was no one else at our table. My heart beat so hard it made my eardrums throb.

I heard it again: *What about a mission?* I tried to shove the thought to the side, but it wouldn't stay there.

Dr. Wallace stood up. "I will pursue the necessary paperwork." He picked up his plate and cup. "Where is the nearest trash receptacle?"

I pointed to the opposite side of the room with my right hand—the hand with the missing pinky. I'd lost that pinky in the eighth grade because I ignored Dr. Wallace's instructions during a field trip and tried to pick up a water moccasin.

Dr. Wallace noticed my hand. "Our last course together ended tragically. This time, however, you are more mature. You will have a greater appreciation for the fundamentals of research." His face cracked into a stiff smile. "I am eager to have you again as my pupil."

"Thanks, Dr. Wallace. I appreciate your help."

As he walked away, my ego floated right out of the chair; then—

What about a mission?

I could hear the air hissing out of my deflating dream. This wasn't fair. Couldn't I go to college first and *then* go on a mission? I'd go right after graduation. It shouldn't matter *when* I served a mission as long as I served one.

I smacked myself in the forehead. What was I doing? That was the same thing Dani had said about marrying in the temple. I sighed. Still, I didn't want to burn all my bridges. Who knew what could happen?

I got up and dumped my plate and cup in the trash, then followed the other well-wishers outside to see the Wallace family off. Melonhead was waiting for me in the parking lot.

"I have to go." He nodded toward the moving van.

"Knoxville isn't that far," I lied. "Just six and a half hours away."

"I know."

"We'll keep in touch."

Melonhead sniffed. "I want to know when you get your mission call. You'll be the first one to know when I get mine."

I felt my face turn red. "I'll call you."

Melonhead's voice was soft and reflective. "Thanks for teaching me about the gospel. It means a lot to me." He glanced back at his family. "I hope someday it will mean something to them too."

Behind us, my mother was embracing Cassiopeia. I would never have imagined the two would end up good friends. But Melonhead and I were friends from the moment we met. He was an easy person to get along with. And he was always honest—a quality I wished I had. I figured now was a good time to start emulating him. "Thanks for all the times you told me the truth, even when I didn't want to hear it."

The U-Haul engine roared. Melonhead's blue eyes filled with tears. He blinked hard, trying not to cry. I hoped I wasn't that obvious.

He held out his hand. "Good-bye, Kev."

My stomach felt hollow in spite of all the cake, punch, and nuts in it. I gripped Melonhead's hand tight, hoping this would not be the last time I'd see my friend.

"We don't have to say good-bye. We'll see each other again. Maybe we'll be in the same mission."

We wrapped our arms around each other. His dark suit coat was stiff and warm from the sun. For an instant I sensed that Melonhead would be a powerful missionary. Then, like always, he said what I wished I'd said first.

"I love you, Kevin."

I swallowed hard. "I love you too, Melonhead."

He patted my back, and we broke our brotherly embrace. We looked at each other's tear-streaked faces and burst out laughing.

"See you in the mission field, Elder Kirk."
"I'll be watching for you, Elder Melon."

Chapter Two

My parents and I had moved to Armadillo, Arkansas, when I was in the seventh grade. My mom had just graduated with a degree in mortuary science, and she and my father decided they wanted to start a family business. So they bought the Paramount Funeral Home, and from that moment on, death has been a part of my everyday life.

I didn't like it at first—living around dead people—but you get used to it. Before we moved to the Paramount, I'd never seen a corpse. But I learned quickly that dead bodies are nothing like what you see in horror movies. There has to be someone to take care of them until they're buried or cremated—that's why morticians are so important.

I also learned that death really does scare some people—but not for the same reasons death is scary in the movies. Death is scary when you don't know that there's more to life than what we see, or when you don't know that there is a reason *why* people have to die sooner or later. And it doesn't seem to bother most of us that our bodies can't live forever, though we often wish the people we love most could.

I guess that's the most important thing I learned at the Paramount: we think death is sad, but God doesn't. It's something He planned for us to experience. I learned this from Cletus McCulley, the dead fisherman who was our first customer at the Paramount, and from an old high priest named Herb Conrad, who will always be my best fishing buddy. I learned it when my grandma died during my freshman year of high school. I learned it from my church—The Church of Jesus Christ of Latter-day Saints— and from my early-morning seminary teacher, Sister Hooper.

Knowing that death is inevitable doesn't make it any less painful. When Grandma died, it still hurt. But it helps me to know that God has more in store for us—and the ones we love—after we die.

Dani Carter was the first friend I made when my family moved to Armadillo. She quickly became my best friend, and—I have to admit— there've been times when I've wondered what it would be like to be married to her.

I thought about it during Dr. Wallace and Cassiopeia's wedding that late summer day. I thought about it again a few weeks later. We'd gone to the Cow Palace. It was the night before the first day of our senior year of high school, and I'd bought her a Lean Cow Pattie with low-fat cheese and a side salad with house dressing. As I watched her eat, I was certain there was no other girl who could steal my heart while nibbling on a Cow Pattie. And most recently I thought about it as she rode with me to school after our first day of early-morning seminary.

But now I was sensing that something wasn't right. Dani was changing. They were small changes, but they nagged at me. The comment she made over the summer about having a "real" wedding was just the beginning. That wasn't like Dani at all. And another thing—before Melonhead moved, the three of us were inseparable. Now I felt more alone than I did when I first moved to Armadillo. With Melonhead gone, Dani and I were the only two Latter-day Saints at Sherman County High, and we needed to stick together. But once school started it was like she made up excuses to avoid spending time with me.

We should have been closer than ever, but instead we were drifting apart. Or, to be more precise, Dani was drifting away from *me*. A good example of that was the day she got reprimanded for not following the dress code. I tried to warn her, but she wouldn't listen.

"Don't you think your shorts are a bit . . . um . . . short?" I asked.

Dani twirled so I could get the 360° view. "You like 'em?"

I didn't answer.

Her face reddened—not with shame, but with anger. "I paid good money for these shorts. Everyone else is wearing them."

"Look around. No one else's shorts are as short as yours."

"You just haven't looked closely enough. My shorts aren't as short as some of the others I've seen."

"They're so short your underwear is showing."

"It's supposed to," Dani said, but she reached behind and tucked them into place anyway. Then all at once her eyes widened. "You think I'm too fat to wear these shorts, don't you?"

I walked her to a corner of the lobby where we could talk privately. "You look—" I stalled, not sure if I wanted to tell her what I was really thinking.

Dani held her breath.

"It's really awkward to say. I mean, you're a girl."

Dani crossed her arms and glared at me. "Tell me. I can take it."

"It's hard not to stare at you." I spoke as quickly as I could, hoping to get it over with. "And I don't like the way other guys are staring at you. It's like you're advertising." I brushed my hand through my short dark hair. "I think when I look at you, I should see you and not your body."

Right then Hunter Rockwell, the senior class jock and number one girl-chaser, decided to interrupt our conversation.

"Hey there, cutie." He nudged Dani with his elbow. "Nice shorts."

Dani sneered at me. "I'm glad somebody likes them."

Hunter proceeded to mesmerize Dani with his stories about how he'd broken three fingers at football camp and had been voted Mr. Sherman County Football three years in a row. When I couldn't stomach any more, I slipped away to search for my first period class. I passed Mr. Schweitzer, the assistant principal. He was headed for the lobby.

The next time I saw Dani was in fourth hour trig. She still had on her Sherman County Seniors Rule T-shirt. But she also had on a pair of baggy gray sweats instead of her shorts.

"Schweitzer caught me. Are you happy now?" She walked past my desk and slumped into her seat.

I didn't turn around. I figured if she saw me grinning, it would only make her madder.

School wasn't the only challenge. Early-morning seminary started a week after school began, and even on the first day of class, Dani was downright belligerent.

Sister Hooper was surprised by Dani's change in behavior, but she was patient with her during the first week of seminary. By the second week, she was visibly frustrated. That's because Dani was doing homework, painting her nails, plucking her eyebrows, and reading *Cosmo Girl* during class.

We were on our third week of seminary and had started section six of the Doctrine and Covenants the day Dani decided to give herself a pedicure. Sister Hooper tried to pretend she could carry on with the lesson. But after Dani finished the second coat of Richly Red on her left toes, Sister Hooper lost it.

"Danielle Carter, I've had enough." Sister Hooper turned and erased everything she'd written on the whiteboard. "I've tried being nice to you. I've tried to overlook your behavior. But painting your toenails in class is too much." She stepped into her kitchen and came back in the room with her cordless phone. "I'm calling your mother."

Dani shrugged her shoulders and brushed more Richly Red on her right toes.

Fifteen minutes later, Sister Carter showed up. "I'll take Dani to school this morning," she said to me.

"I don't mind taking her."

Sister Carter watched Dani blow across the wet nail polish. "No, I believe we need time to talk."

When seminary was over, I left Sister Hooper's house and drove to school. At lunch, I waited for Dani, but she never showed. When I ran into Tiff Beeny, one of Dani's friends, I asked if she'd seen her. Tiff said Dani hadn't attended any of her classes that day.

The next morning Dani acted like her old self. She read aloud the passages Sister Hooper asked her to, and she didn't appear to be bored or distracted. When class was over, she tossed her backpack in the back of the S-10, and we took off for school.

"I missed you at school yesterday," I told her. "I looked for you all day."

"I spent the day with my mom."

When we got to school, she jumped out of the truck and ran off, leaving me alone in the parking lot. Later that morning I saw Hunter

Rockwell in the hall. A group of girls hovered around him like flies around a dinner plate. Dani was walking several steps behind Hunter. She was carrying his books.

What was wrong with her?

I fumed the rest of the day. When I got home I parked the S-10 in the hearse garage. I got out, slammed the truck door, and kicked the front tire.

Granddad was building shelves to hang on the garage walls. "Better be nice to the old Chevy. She's on her last legs. She needs you to fix her, not kick her when she's down."

"At least I can fix the truck," I said. "Girls don't want your help. They get in a mess, and then when you try to help them fix their problems, it makes 'em mad."

Granddad measured the plank of wood and marked it. "I hate to tell you this, but I'm seventy and I still haven't got women figured out." Then he measured the wood and marked it again.

I stuffed my hands in my pockets. "They're so frustrating. They know what's right, yet they'll do what's wrong to get what they want—even when what they want isn't right for them."

Granddad chuckled. "You're talking about people in general—not just girls." He picked up the power saw and motioned for me to hold the board. When I had a firm grip on it, he set the saw on the mark and turned it on. The metal blade rang as it sliced through the board. When the severed end hit the concrete floor, he turned off the saw and set it down.

"Look," I insisted, "I know the difference between right and wrong. I'm not going to run around half naked just to get a girl to look at me. I'm not going to do whatever a girl wants just to get her to like me."

Granddad laid another board on the sawhorses and measured it twice. "Sometimes when we want something badly enough, we'll do foolish things to get it. That goes for men as well as women, so don't get the idea you're too smart to be stupid."

"But she's old enough to know better."

"Age doesn't matter. Even old geezers like me who should know better can get messed up." He nodded to the end of the board, and I held it while he sawed.

Granddad finished cutting the board. Then Marshall came in and handed me a ten. "I need you to run to Woods. Marcy's dying for a malt."

"What about the O'Connell visitation? Doesn't Mom need my help?"

"I'll take your place as greeter. I tried to convince Marcy to wait. I told her I'd get her a malt tonight, but you can't argue with a pregnant woman."

"I don't think you can argue with any woman, period." I took the ten and got back in the truck.

Woods Pharmacy was an old-timey drugstore and soda fountain in the heart of historic downtown Armadillo, sandwiched between the offices of the Armadillo *Courier* and Higgenbotham's Antiques and What-Nots. Besides all the modern drugstore items, Woods also housed a small museum of medicines old people used "back in the day" as Granddad liked to say—stuff like Carter's Little Liver Pills and antique bottles of castor oil.

The soda fountain was similar to the ones you see in the old black-and-white movies. You could sit on a barstool at the counter and watch the soda jerks whip up your favorite concoction. Metal tables for two invited visitors to stop and share a root beer float. A wrought iron staircase spiraled up to the roof, where customers could sit and enjoy a hot fudge sundae under the stars.

When I got to Woods, the pharmacy half of the store was busy. The only customers at the soda fountain were an elderly gentleman and his wife. They were sitting at a corner table, conversing over a banana split.

I sat down at the counter and rang the bell. Dani emerged from the back room.

"I didn't know you were working tonight. I thought you were only going to work through the summer."

"Mr. Woods said he could use me if I was willing to work. He doesn't make me work too late at night. And I like having the extra money."

I laid the ten on the counter. "Marshall sent me to pick up a malt for Marcy."

After Dani gave me the change, she poured the ingredients for the malt in the mixer.

"You look cute in your uniform." I wanted to say that at least it covered her body, but I didn't.

"Thanks. This is to-go, right?" She turned on the mixer.

I nodded.

She turned it off and poured the malt into a Styrofoam cup. "Whipped cream?"

I nodded again, and Dani squirted a huge dollop on top.

I pointed to the jar of maraschino cherries on the counter. "Marcy likes those."

Dani positioned the cherry on top of the whipped cream and put a domed plastic lid on the cup. "How's she feeling?"

"Her cravings are driving Marshall up the wall. Last week she made him drive to Gleason for pickled bologna."

Dani scrunched her face in disgust. "I'd be driving to get *away* from pickled bologna, not driving somewhere to buy it."

I leaned onto the counter. Dani and I were having an easy conversation and enjoying each other's company. It was just like old times.

Dani pulled up a stool and sat down across from me. "So are you going to the homecoming game?"

"I'm not into football. I like baseball better."

Dani picked up a straw, tore the paper off, and twirled it between her fingers. "I'd like to go." Her voice was low and soft, but she didn't look me in the eyes. "I think Mr. Woods would let me off work that night."

My chest grew warm and my heartbeat quickened. I studied Dani's face. I knew every eyelash and every freckle, the curve of her jaw and how the arch of one eyebrow was slightly higher than the other.

The only excuse I can give for what I said next is that I was under her influence. I loved her and I wanted her to be happy. "I know it's kind of early to ask—homecoming's not until October—"

Dani gasped and her face flushed.

I swallowed hard. "Um, I'd like to take you to homecoming—that is, if you'd let me."

Dani's mouth burst into a humongous smile. To me, it was like the heavens had opened.

"You'd take me?" she asked as if my proposal was too good to be true.

"Of course."

"Oh Kevin, you're wonderful!" She leaned over the counter and flung her arms around my neck.

I put my arms around her too and savored the moment. The elderly couple behind us clapped their congratulations.

She released me, but the scent of her perfume remained on my skin. I took a deep breath.

"Thanks for asking me," Dani said.

I took my keys from my pocket. "I'd better get this malt to Marcy before it melts."

"We'll have a great time at the dance. I promise."

"I always have a great time when I'm with you."

Dani's cheeks glowed in response.

I had to watch the speedometer on the way home. My foot was heavy on the gas, and I kept going over the speed limit. I couldn't get Dani—or the joy of feeling her arms around me—off my mind.

Chapter Three

After I asked Dani to the homecoming dance, she couldn't stop talking about it. Every morning at seminary, she quizzed me about what I was going to wear and what I thought she should wear. On the way to school she talked about corsages. And on Sundays while we were at church, she talked about where we'd go out to eat and how we'd pose for our photos.

It only took a few days of this for me to get tired of hearing about what we were going to wear, eat, do, etc. But I was determined not to let Dani know that. More than anything, I wanted her to be happy. I didn't care if she ever quit talking about homecoming. If going to a homecoming dance was all Dani needed to be happy, I was going to make sure she got there and that every dream she had for that night would come true.

A couple of weeks before homecoming, I got an envelope in the mail from Dr. Wallace. Inside was an application for Nelson-Barrett University, along with a sticky note that said,

> *Looking forward to seeing you next fall.*
> *Please list me as one of your references.*
>
> *Dr. A. L. W.*
>
> *P. S. Do not mark Wedgewood Hall as*
> *your housing choice. The plumbing is*
> *insufficient; the toilets have a reputation*
> *for overflowing.*

So Dr. Wallace wasn't kidding when he said he wanted to help me get into Nelson-Barrett U. I decided right then I needed to get serious about college.

But what about a mission?

I put the application back in the envelope, not sure what I should do.

I sat on the bed and flipped the envelope over and over in my hands. I didn't like feeling confused. I glanced up at my calendar on the wall.

The ACT was coming up in a few days, so I decided to do some online practice tests to take my mind off my dilemma. I'd just sat down at the computer when I heard the phone ring. Mom came in a few minutes later, her eyes as big as Moon Pies. "Do you know where your father is?"

"He's in the chapel, working on the casket stand."

Next thing I knew, Mom was gone. I heard her running down the stairs; it sounded like she was taking the steps two at a time. All was quiet for a while after that.

I was halfway through the science-reasoning portion of the practice test when my parents thundered back up the stairs. I went to see what all the commotion was about and found Mom frantically trying to straighten up the apartment.

"Arlice, go put on a suit and tie." Mom grabbed the dirty paper plates off the side table and stuffed them in the trash. "And brush your teeth too."

Dad wrung his hands as he meandered around the den. "Just because Daniel's coming over doesn't mean I have to get dressed up. He comes over here all the time."

Mom stopped in her tracks and eyed Dad. "Then why are you so nervous?"

"I'm not."

"Are too. You don't pace the floor every time the branch president visits."

"What's going on?" I asked.

Mom clenched the front of my shirt with both hands. "You have to help me get things straightened up," she pleaded. "And tell your father to put on a suit and tie."

I picked up the stack of newspapers beside the couch. "Dad looks fine. Besides, he's been working downstairs in the funeral parlor. He'll stink up his suit if he puts it on without taking a shower first."

Dad looked relieved. "Thank you, son."

"Well, here." Mom reached into the box of stuff she kept for Lily B and took out a handful of baby wipes. "Clean yourself off with these."

"But Mom, he'll smell like a baby!"

"No, he won't." Mom motioned to Dad. "Wipe, Arlice. Hurry!"

Dad was so nervous he did as he was told.

I sighed and took the newspapers out to our recycle box.

We'd barely finished the emergency cleanup when the sound of heavy footsteps echoed out on the deck. Someone knocked on the kitchen door.

Dad smoothed his moustache and brushed his hands over his nearly bald head.

Mom took a deep breath and opened the door. "Good evening, Daniel." She motioned for President Carter to come in. "And welcome, President Kensington."

The stake president? What was he doing here?

"I hope this isn't an inconvenient time," President Kensington said. "I was in Armadillo on business and thought we might as well meet now instead of Sunday."

Dad swallowed hard. "We're glad you stopped by." I wasn't so sure Dad meant what he said. He looked ready to jump out of his skin.

Mom offered her hand. "I'm Freda." She gestured toward me. "And this is our son, Kevin."

President Kensington wrinkled his nose. "Do you have a baby?"

Mom picked up Lily B's latest portrait. "We have a granddaughter—Lily—at least we call her our granddaughter. Her mother is like a daughter to us and so—"

Dad still had a baby wipe in his hand. He stuffed it in his pocket. "We have a granddaughter and another grandchild on the way."

Mom nudged Dad. "Why don't you give the stake president a tour of the Paramount?" Then, instead of letting him do it, she stood in the middle of the room and announced, "This is our apartment where we live, and this," Mom gestured as if she were one of the stage models on *The Price Is Right*, "is our living area. We live here."

President Kensington raised an eyebrow. "How convenient."

Mom glowed and her gestures became more animated. "This is the perfect place to live, although it *is* a bit crowded. As you can see, there's no dead space here—"

Dad rolled his eyes. "Freda—"

"The parlor—I mean the business—is downstairs." She nudged Dad again, this time harder. "Why don't you show him the chapel?"

President Carter spoke up. "President Kensington could do the interview there."

Interview?

Dad wrung his hands again. "Follow me." He led them to the door. "Watch your step. The stairs are steep."

As soon as they were downstairs, Mom flopped onto the couch.

"What's going on?" I asked.

"All I know is the stake president is interviewing your father."

Big deal. "I'm going back to my room."

Mom rubbed her eyes with one hand and shooed me away with the other.

I tried to resume my practice test, but I'd let the computer idle for too long and the session had timed out. I had to start over. I'd answered ten reading-comprehension questions when

President Carter came back and asked Mom to come downstairs.

An hour later, I was still working on the practice test, and my parents were still talking to the stake president. I yawned and stretched. The questions on the screen blurred together and my brain hurt. I'd had enough practice for one night. My cat, Lima Bean, leapt onto my desk and walked over my keyboard. I wiggled the mouse, and he pawed at the pointer as it moved across the monitor.

"You're shedding all over my keyboard." I put him on the bed, and he tried his best to curse me with his unblinking green eyes.

"What do you think is going on down there?" I asked.

Lima Bean picked up his right front leg in response and casually raked his tongue over his paw.

"Do you even care?"

Lima Bean flopped onto his back and stretched. He twisted his middle so that his front paws stuck up in the air while his back paws were flat on the bed. It looked like he was unscrewing his top half from his bottom half.

I took that as a no.

When Mom and Dad returned, they were alone. "Let's have a snack," Dad said. He patted his stomach. It didn't sound hollow to me.

Mom got the paper plates. Dad opened the refrigerator.

"Mmm. Macaroni and cheese." He set the bowl on the table. "Did we eat all the banana pudding?"

"Where's President Carter?" I asked. "Where's President Kensington?"

Dad picked up a plate of leftover pork chops and, after he lifted the aluminum foil covering, sniffed to make sure they hadn't been in the fridge too long.

"What about olives?" Mom asked.

"Yup. We got some—ooh, looky here!" Dad lifted a plastic bowl as if it were a first-place trophy. "Fried okra!"

"Didn't we just eat dinner?" I asked.

"Dinner was hours ago," Dad insisted. He checked his watch. "It's after nine now."

Mom grabbed the olive jar. "I love olives. Especially those little red things they stuff 'em with."

"Pimentos," Dad said. He popped open the okra bowl. "You reckon this would be good heated up in the microwave?"

My parents were absorbed in their food—or at least they were pretending to be. "What happened with the stake president?"

Mom shoved the bread basket in my face. "Corn muffin?"

I pushed it away. "He had to be here for a reason."

Dad dumped a lump of macaroni on his plate. "I love cold macaroni. It's as good out of the fridge as it is hot out of the pot."

Mom jumped from her chair as if she'd had a sudden revelation. She opened the refrigerator and searched the bottom shelf. "Potato salad! I knew we had some left." She handed the bowl to Dad.

"Mmm. Marcy makes the best potato salad. I'm glad you remembered it." He dug into it as if it would be the last time he'd ever eat any.

It was obvious my parents weren't going to tell me what happened. I held my hand up in the air. "Fine. I don't have to know what's going on."

Mom slapped a chop in my hand. "Have some pork, dear."

"Gimme one of those," Dad said through a mouthful of macaroni.

Mom tossed him a pork chop, then ladled out some olives. They rolled around on her plate like green eyeballs. "Kevin, grab us some soda. Make sure it's diet."

I put the pork chop on a plate, wiped the grease from my hand, and got three cans of diet soda from the fridge. I figured I might as well have a snack too.

"Maybe we should call Granddad," I said and helped myself to some cold okra. "He likes leftovers."

"Granddad's playing bingo at the Elks Lodge again," Dad said. He popped an olive in his mouth, then grimaced. "This one still has a pit. I hope I didn't crack a tooth." He wrapped the pit in a napkin and set it aside.

"Wish we could get him to come to church with us," Mom sawed her stiff pork chop into bite-size pieces. "I worry about him. He plays bingo all the time. He needs something more constructive to do."

I didn't agree. "He's always repairing something around here. He probably likes getting a break from the funeral home."

Dad salted his potato salad. "He'd be a big help to the branch."

I split a corn muffin and slathered it with butter. "Have you ever asked him to come to church?"

Dad stopped chewing. "No." He turned to Mom. "Have you?"

Mom's eyes widened. "I thought you had."

"Well," I said as I smushed the halves of my corn muffin back together, "I guess someone needs to."

"Maybe he'll come this Sunday to see you sustained," Mom said to Dad.

Dad nodded in agreement.

Ah-ha! So this was what the food frenzy was all about. "Sustained to what?"

Dad gnawed on a pork chop bone and didn't answer.

Mom patted Dad's arm. "The stake president issued your father a new calling in church."

Dad gnawed harder on the bone.

Mom popped the top on Dad's soda. "He's going to be a counselor in the branch presidency. It'll be a lot of responsibility, but your father can handle it."

Dad dropped the bone and started on the okra.

"We can't tell anyone about this." Mom gave me a stern look. "Not until after he's sustained on Sunday."

When I went to bed, I thought about what Mom had said—how Dad would have a lot of responsibility in his new calling. She was sure he could handle it. I wasn't sure Dad felt the same.

Lima Bean woke me up a little after one in the morning. He was in my bed, pouncing on a twist tie and flipping it in the air with his paws. I sat up and rubbed my eyes. Outside my window I could see that the sky was clear and the stars were exceptionally bright.

Something was moving in the grassy area between the parking lot and the woods. I went to the window to check it out.

It was my father.

I put on my shoes, pulled on a hoodie, and went outside to see what he was up to.

Dad didn't even know I was there until I tapped him on the arm. He jumped. "What are you tryin' to do? Give me a heart attack?" He tightened the belt on his robe.

"Sorry. I saw you out here pacing and—"

"Never mind."

He resumed pacing. I walked beside him, matching my steps to his. He didn't talk. I didn't either. By the time Granddad showed up, we'd worn a nice path in the grass.

"What in blazes are you doing out here?" Granddad asked.

"Pacing," I said.

"Don't you know it's one thirty in the morning?"

"Yeah," I said. "It *is* kinda late."

Dad sped up. I darted forward to catch up with him.

Granddad joined the silent march. The three of us walked and walked and walked, back and forth and back and forth.

"Three guys, outside in the middle of the night, marching in their pajamas—what would Grandma say if she could see us?" I asked.

Granddad chuckled. "She'd say, 'Hang on and let me get my robe. I want to walk with you.'"

"She'd bring us hot chocolate too," I added.

"Your mother, on the other hand—"

"If Mom wakes up and sees us, she'll be mad. Her voice'll get all squeaky." I tightened my throat and spoke in my best high-pitched Mom voice: "It's the middle of the night! You'll catch pneumonia and die!"

Dad came to an abrupt stop. "So my nerves are shot and I can't sleep! I didn't ask you to come out here! I can walk in my own backyard by myself any time I want!"

Granddad hitched up his pajama pants. "What's the matter, son?"

Dad abandoned his straight-line march and began wandering in circles. "I don't know if I can do it."

Granddad scratched his head. "Do what?"

"It's a big commitment. My head says, 'Arlice, you can't do this. You're not smart enough.' But I couldn't say no. How *could* I say no?"

Granddad frowned. "I have no idea what you're talking about."

Dad stopped and put his hands on his temples as if he had a headache. "I'm going to be a counselor in the branch presidency at church. I'll have to go to meetings and interview people and conduct services and—"

"That's no different than your work at the Paramount."

Dad crossed his arms and sighed deep.

"Yeah, Dad," I added. "You meet with people to plan services. You've gone to mortician meetings before. You've even conducted funerals when there wasn't a preacher available."

"But it's not the same," Dad said. "This is *church* service."

Granddad put his hand on Dad's shoulder. "You're not serving the Church, son. You're serving God."

Dad's jaw dropped. I was amazed too. I'd never heard Granddad talk like that.

Granddad looked Dad in the eye. "Why do you go to church?"

"Because I believe what the Church teaches."

"Let's try again. Who does your church teach about?"

"God and Jesus Christ," I interjected.

Granddad kept his eyes on Dad. "Kevin, let your father answer. He's the confused one."

Dad pawed his foot in the grass. "I go to church to learn about God. Is that better?"

Granddad held up his index finger, signaling that he was ready to make his point. "If you serve the Church, you'll never do enough. The Church will always need more. The people will always need more. But if your position is to serve God—well, that's a whole 'nother can of beans."

"Your advice isn't helping," Dad said. I could tell he was losing patience.

Granddad thought for a second before he spoke. "If you serve the people, you'll be influenced by how the people judge your service. There'll always be someone who's not satisfied with what you do."

Dad sighed. "I *am* supposed to serve people."

Granddad pointed his finger again, this time more adamantly. "You're *supposed* to serve God."

"I don't see the difference." Dad stuck his hands in his pockets. For a second he reminded me of a little kid.

"Listen, son. God knows when you're giving Him your best—and that's all He wants. People? You can give 'em all you've got, and they still won't be satisfied. They'll complain because you didn't give 'em what they want. And you'll get discouraged and think you're a failure."

Granddad pointed to the sky as if his words were written in the stars. "God, on the other hand, isn't going to expect something out of you without showing you how to get it done. He doesn't want any of us to fail. He wants to make good soldiers out of us. I mean, if He kicked out everybody that didn't polish their boots right the first time, he'd have an awfully small platoon."

Dad wiped his eyes.

"That's cool, Granddad," I said. "Where'd you learn that?"

"The army." Granddad strutted ahead of us. "If your drill sergeant is happy, that's all you need to worry about."

I couldn't help but grin at Granddad's logic.

The three of us started pacing again. We walked in silence for a long time.

"Dad?" my father said to his father.

"What?"

"I want you to be there when I'm sustained."

"Nothing would please me more. Do I have to wear a tie?"

"I'll loan you one."

"I haven't worn a tie since your mother's funeral." Granddad groaned. "Oh well. I guess wearing a tie once every four years isn't going to kill me."

I yawned. "Now that that's settled, I'm going back to bed. G'night."

"Good night, Kev," Dad said.

"Good night, Kev," Granddad echoed.

I went up to my room and took off my shoes and my hoodie. Before I crawled back in bed, I glanced out the window. Dad and Granddad were walking side by side. They were so much alike on the outside—and more similar on the inside than I'd ever realized.

Chapter Four

On homecoming night I put on a white dress shirt, green striped tie, and black suit. I stood in front of the mirror to check myself out. Tall, clean-shaven, broad shoulders, dark hair combed just right. I felt pretty smug. I looked just as good as Hunter Rockwell. And I'd make sure Dani had such a good time at the dance that she wouldn't give Hunter Rockwell a second thought. Then out of the corner of my eye I saw a missionary nametag on my breast pocket that said ELDER KIRK. I gasped.

I put my hand to the pocket. Nothing.

I glanced up and stared into my reflection. My dark, nearly-black eyes gawked back at me. Shaken, I grabbed the keys to the truck and left.

When I arrived at Dani's, President Carter answered the door. He let me in and invited me to have a seat.

"We'll be right there," Sister Carter called out from the other room.

I entered the den where Dani's little brothers, Dylan and Derek, were battling on the couch. When they saw me they giggled and made kissy-kissy noises. I gave them my meanest piercing stare and settled into the recliner to wait for Dani.

Something hit the side of my head and stuck there. I peeled it off. It was a chunk of banana. I wiped the goo off my head, but as soon as I put the handkerchief back in my pocket, they hit me with more banana.

"Cut it out," I growled. "Aren't you guys too old for that?"

"Aren't you guys too old for that?" Dylan mimicked. Then he and Derek collapsed into hysterics.

I wondered if I had been that obnoxious when I was nine years old.

"What are you boys up to?" President Carter peeked in the door. His face was stern. "Why do I smell bananas?"

"There must be monkeys in the room," Dani said as she walked around her father and to the recliner. She had on a silky brown dress and a matching jacket. She looked so elegant. My old black suit suddenly felt shaggy and worn. I wished I'd at least bought a new tie for the occasion.

I stood up and carefully removed the corsage from its plastic box. "I hope you like this. Mom helped me pick it out. I tried to get something in school colors that would still match your outfit."

"I'll help you pin it on," Sister Carter said to Dani. She took the corsage and pinned it to Dani's lapel. "There. Isn't that cute?" The corsage was an orange mum that had been forced into an oval shape, with a piece of black pipe cleaner across the top to make it resemble a football.

"Gimme a *K,* gimme an *I,* gimme an *S, S, S,*" Dylan sang as Dani's parents snapped a photo of us. Derek cackled beside him.

Dani scowled. "Cut it out, Doofus."

President Carter shushed the boys. "I want you home by midnight, Dani. Call if you're going to be late." Then he turned to me. "I trust you to bring her home at the appropriate time."

Why was I nervous all of a sudden? "I've got a cell phone. I'll call if there's a problem."

Dani dragged me to the door. "We'll be fine. See you at midnight."

I held the door for Dani and she climbed in the truck. When I got in, I reached over and wiggled her seat belt buckle.

"What are you doing?" she asked.

"Checking to make sure you're buckled in. I don't want anything to happen to you."

Dani pushed my hand away. "Good grief, Kevin. I don't need you to take care of me. I can take care of myself."

Embarrassed, I buckled up and started the truck. "You want to go to the Cow Palace and get a burger or something before the game?"

"No, let's go now—I want to get a good seat."

"I didn't know you were interested in football."

"Guess I've got school spirit." Dani made cheerleader motions with her arms. "Go, go, go Armadillos!"

I laughed. "I'll buy you a corn dog at the concession stand then."

"How about two? I'm starving."

Dani chatted all the way to the athletic complex. She talked about her classes, about the colleges she planned to apply to, and about her job at the soda fountain. It was just like old times, like when we were in junior high. I didn't want the ride to end.

At the stadium, Dani insisted we sit as close to the field as possible. I was sure we'd have a hard time finding a seat since the game was about to start. But we made our way to the front row and found a couple of empty spots close to the thirty-yard line on the Sherman County side.

I didn't care for football, but it was hard not to get absorbed into the energy of the crowd. I bought Dani a pair of pom poms and a banner for myself so we could cheer along with the other Sherman County fans.

Hunter was out on the field, doing what quarterbacks do—being the hero. He made a pass—the crowd roared. He ran for a first down—the cheerleaders went wild. He scored a touchdown, then another, then another—and soon the pep band was drowned out by the yells of the fans in the stands.

I had to admit, Hunter was a great football player. When the game was over, Sherman County had humiliated the competition 36 to 0.

Dani and I left the stadium and made our way to the dimly lit gym for the homecoming dance. The music thumped so hard against the brick walls that I thought I could see the mortar cracking.

"Want some soda?"

"No." Dani seemed afraid to take her gaze away from one of the side doors—the one that led to the boys' locker room.

A gang of girls gathered around Dani, and for fifteen minutes they compared outfits and gossiped about everybody else's. It was one of the lamest conversations I'd ever heard.

When I couldn't take any more, I tapped Dani on the shoulder. "Are you sure you don't want some soda?"

Dani thought for a second. "Maybe a diet soda."

"Be right back."

There were two self-serve soft drink machines, one on each side of the refreshment table. I poured Dani a diet soda and was contemplating whether I should get some cake when the gym exploded with applause.

The door to the boys' locker room had opened.

The pep band began to play "Our Boys Will Shine Tonight."

Then, like a herd of orange buffalos, the Sherman County football team thundered into the gym. The players ran a lap around the perimeter of the gym, beating their chests and doing Tarzan yells. The crowd cheered as each player's name blasted through the PA system.

All the players, that is, but one.

The next thing I knew, there was an anticipatory drum roll, followed by the melodramatic announcer: "And nooooooow, tonight's mooooost vaaaaaaluable player—"

All heads turned to the locker room doors.

"Huuuuuunterrrrr Rockwell!"

Hunter burst through the doors. The roar from the crowd was deafening. The jocks gave him high fives as he zoomed past. The girls screamed like he was a rock star.

Where was Dani? I abandoned the cake and pushed my way through the swarm. I stood on my tiptoes and stretched my neck, hoping to catch a glimpse of her in the crowd.

When I saw her, my heart sank to the soles of my freshly polished shoes. She had followed the rest of Hunter's groupies to the center of the gym. When I finally caught up with her, I was sweaty and the ice in her drink had almost melted.

I handed her the cup. "Sorry I took so long. It was hard to get through all the commotion."

"Forget it," Dani said. There was a hint of annoyance in her voice. She tugged at the sleeve of my jacket. "Come on. If we don't hurry we'll never get through!" She dragged me through the crowd until we reached the spot where Hunter stood. He was surrounded by the girls Dani had gossiped with earlier.

"What are you doing?" I broke free from her desperate grip. "It's too crowded here."

"Hunter played a great game tonight. Don't you want to congratulate him?"

"Not especially."

"It'll be rude if we don't."

All around us, people were jostling to get to the Most Valuable Player. Someone bumped my arm, and Dani's soda spilled all over the front of my suit. I let the cup fall to the floor and peeled off my sweaty, soda-stained jacket. "Let's get out of here. It's hot, and I'm getting claustrophobic."

"I won't leave until I talk to Hunter," Dani said firmly. She took off her jacket too, revealing the strapless top she had on underneath. She threw the jacket at me. "Hold this. I'll be back." She dove into the writhing crowd and disappeared.

I fought my way toward the bleachers, and when I found an empty spot on the front row, I sat down and waited for Dani to come back.

I waited.

I waited some more. Fifteen minutes. Thirty minutes. An hour.

After an hour and fifteen minutes, I realized I had become invisible. People walked by without speaking. They stood in front of me and had conversations as if they didn't know I was there. Some walked up and dumped their trash onto the chair right next to me without even acknowledging my presence.

Dani's corsage was in bad shape. The mum stem had snapped and the head was droopy. The pipe-cleaner laces had fallen off. Some of the petals were missing. I shifted Dani's jacket from my left arm to my right. The corsage pin pricked my hand—the one with the missing pinky— and a small spot of blood oozed up from my palm. I wiped it on my leg. I didn't want it to stain her jacket.

The clock on the gym wall said eleven thirty. The crowd was dancing, still going strong. I didn't see Dani anywhere.

Then I saw Hunter heading to the doors on the opposite side of the gym.

Dani ran up, said something to Hunter, and backed away.

Hunter seized her arm.

I squeezed my fists tight. Hunter was a football player, but I could take him. I rose from the bench.

Dani moved closer to Hunter. She smiled up at him.

She tucked her arm through his. Then they left the dance—together.

Everyone at school knew I'd brought Dani to homecoming, and now everyone knew she'd dumped me at homecoming to leave with the star quarterback of the Sherman County North football team.

I sat down and put my head in my hands. A lump swelled in my throat, and it wouldn't go away. I was glad I hadn't eaten any cake. I would have thrown it up.

Eleven forty-five. I folded Dani's jacket—and mine—over my arm and exited the gym. As I walked to the parking lot, a pair of halogen headlights blinded me. I held my empty arm in front of my face. The lights dimmed.

It was Hunter, behind the wheel of his big SUV. He had one hand on the steering wheel and his other arm around Dani.

She never saw me standing in the road. Her eyes were fixed on Hunter.

When I opened the door of the truck, the interior still smelled like Dani's perfume. I pitched my jacket onto the empty passenger seat. I unpinned Dani's corsage from her jacket and threw it out the window. Then I laid her jacket on top of mine.

It was eleven fifty-six by my watch.

I fingered the passenger's side seat belt buckle. Hunter didn't care if Dani wore her seat belt or not. Heck, he wasn't even wearing his when I saw them together in the SUV.

President Carter had trusted me to take care of his daughter. I'd failed.

Eleven fifty-nine.

My stomach tightened. I had to call him. I didn't want to. Dani would get mad and blame me for getting her into trouble. Then there was the embarrassment of having to admit out loud to someone that I'd been dumped by my date.

I pressed each number slowly and deliberately until I got to the sixth digit. I paused.

I couldn't do it.

I backed out of my parking spot and when I turned around, I saw Dani's battered corsage lying on the asphalt. I put the truck in gear and stepped on the ignition. The tires squealed. I ran over the corsage. I backed up and did it again, but I didn't get the satisfaction I thought I would.

I left the school and headed for the Carters'.

At twelve sixteen I stood on Dani's front porch and handed her jacket over to her father. President Carter didn't say a word when he took it. He didn't have to. The grief in his eyes said more than words ever could.

He held the jacket up to his chest, nodded a silent good night, and closed the door.

I got in the truck and headed for home. The narrow, two-lane country road was deserted and dark. I didn't see the armadillo in my lane until it was too late. The truck rolled over him. I heard the sickening crack as his outer shell was crushed by the front wheels, then the back wheels.

I'd never hit an animal before. Tears scorched my cheeks. I said a silent prayer and hoped that the armadillo had at least died quickly.

When I got home, Mom was on the couch. She'd tried to wait up for me, but sleep won out.

I was glad. She'd have seen my bloodshot eyes and asked a bunch of questions I didn't want to answer. I tiptoed past her to my room.

Lima Bean was snoozing in his usual spot on my bed. When he heard me come in, he yawned, showing off his fanglike teeth. I picked him up and held him close.

"You'll never be an outside cat, Lima Bean. I promise."

I scratched him between his ears. He rolled his head appreciatively, as if to say thank you.

Chapter Five

After Dad became a member of the branch presidency, we learned that the words *sacrifice* and *convenience*—when it comes to church service—rarely get used in the same sentence. He had to go to meetings before the regular Sunday meetings started, he had to stay after church for more meetings, and he had to help the clerks count the tithing and fast-offering donations.

Then there was the Saturday night when we were in the middle of a visitation, and Dad got a call from President Carter.

"Go ahead, Arlice." Mom stuffed the car keys in his hand and practically shoved him out the door. "Kevin and I can handle the crowd."

A group of elderly women had just arrived to pay their respects to Mr. Alphonse Oxnard Beasley. I held the door as the first two entered. They were followed by an especially frail-looking lady in a wheelchair. Dad got behind her and pushed her chair over the threshold.

The woman smacked Dad's hand. "Get your paws off my chair!"

Dad jerked his hand back. "Ow! What'd you do that for?"

"I ain't helpless, boy." She grabbed the wheels and thrust them forward, burning rubber as she skidded across the tile floor to the chapel.

I laughed. "You'd better go before the rest of the Red Hat Society decides to beat you up."

Dad got his briefcase from the office and kissed Mom good-bye. "I'll be back later. Kevin, you mind the store."

"No problem."

When Dad got home that night, it was late and I was asleep. When I woke up Sunday morning, he'd already left for his meetings.

Mom and I made it to church just as the prelude music ended. "Welcome to Fix-Rite," the talking In door welcomed us in its cheery automated voice.

"Oh! I forgot my scriptures!" Mom whispered close to my ear. "Run back out and get them for me."

I groaned. "Can't you get them later?"

"I'm teaching the eight-year-olds today, and I need them before Primary."

I stepped on the Out door mat. "Thank you for shopping at Fix-Rite. Please come again." Everyone turned to see who was leaving.

I ran to the hearse and got Mom's scriptures. Back at the doors, I could see President Carter standing at the lectern. I grimaced as I stepped onto the mat.

The In door opened. "Welcome to Fix-Rite," it said, punctuating its greeting with a pneumatic hiss.

President Carter paused while I slinked into the makeshift chapel. I took my seat next to Mom and tried to ignore the eyes of the elderly women in the front who let me know by their frowns that I'd interrupted the meeting.

After the sacrament was passed, President Carter stood up and adjusted the microphone. "I have an important announcement this morning. I received an exciting phone call this week. The Church has purchased some land here in Sherman County, on the outskirts of Armadillo."

The silence was immediate. Even Dylan and Derek quit punching each other long enough to listen.

Dad shifted in his seat behind the lectern.

President Carter straightened his tie and cleared his throat. "By this time next year, the Armadillo, Arkansas Branch of The Church of

Jesus Christ of Latter-day Saints will be meeting in a brand-new building."

The collective gasp by the small congregation was followed by an outburst of applause not typical of an LDS church service.

President Carter motioned to the crowd. "Let's remember we're in the house of the Lord—even if it is an old hardware store." Then he gave the crowd a broad grin. "However, we *can* be reverent and joyful at the same time."

Mom squeezed my hand. "Isn't this exciting?" she whispered. "We're going to have a real church building to meet in."

"You think they'll let us take the talking doors when we move out?" I joked. "I'll miss going to church at the Fix-Rite."

When everyone settled down, the meeting resumed. The speakers tried to stay focused on their topics, but it was obvious that all anyone wanted to talk about was the new church building.

Dani approached me when it was time to go to Sunday School. "Isn't this great? We're going to have a new building. Too bad it won't get finished before we graduate. We could have seminary here instead of at Sister Hooper's house."

My good mood vanished. Dani hadn't spoken to me since the night she dumped me at homecoming. She was late to seminary every day—so she wouldn't have to talk to me before class, I figured—and she'd stopped riding to school with me afterward. She didn't speak to me in the few classes we had together at school. And when she saw me coming down the hall, she'd turn and go the opposite way.

And now, just because we're getting a new church building, she decides to talk to me?

Baloney.

"I don't know why you'd care," I said.

"What do you mean?"

I could feel my heart pound and break at the same time. But I steeled myself. I stared straight ahead and refused to look her in the eyes. I spoke carefully and deliberately. "You don't care about seminary. You don't care about Church standards. You don't care if you're hurting your parents or your friends. All you care about is what Hunter Rockwell thinks of you."

Dani walked away. She didn't show up for Sunday School.

Marcy and Marshall came over for lunch when Mom and I got home from church.

I put Lily B's booster seat in the chair next to mine and sat her down. She ate her mashed potatoes, then grew annoyed with her peas when they rolled off her spoon. She finally ate them one at a time. Then she arranged her carrots into a small mound.

"Why did you eat your peas and not your carrots?" I asked. "I thought you liked carrots."

"I do. But I want to gib my carrots to Lima Bean."

"Lima Bean doesn't eat carrots. He eats cat food."

"Carrots taste better dan cat food." Lily B gathered the carrots onto her napkin. She folded the napkin around the carrots and put it in her pocket.

"How do you know?"

"I ate some."

"Ate some carrots?"

"No. Cat food."

I took the napkin out of Lily B's pocket. "Don't eat cat food. It'll make you sick."

"Den why do you make Lima Bean eat it?"

"Because he's a cat."

Lily B's face shriveled up. "Dat's *not* fair, Unka Kebin."

Marcy waddled over. "What are you fussing about?"

Lily B tried to answer, but her words were muffled by the damp washcloth Marcy was using to wipe off her mouth.

"She wants to give her carrots to Lima Bean," I said. I put the napkin full of carrots back on the table.

Lily B clenched her fists and kicked. "But—cat—food—tastes—bad! Dat's—not—fair!"

Marcy finished cleaning her up and helped her out of her booster seat. "Cat food tastes bad to you. It doesn't taste bad to the cat."

Lily B snatched the napkin and ran to my room. I watched her through the open door. She crawled onto my bed, opened the napkin, and put the carrots next to Lima Bean.

"I lub you, Lima Bean," Lily B said. "I will gib you my carrots because I lub you so much."

* * *

Two weeks later, the Armadillo *Courier* ran a press release announcing the groundbreaking for our new branch building.

A few days after that, an angry letter to the editor appeared on the opinion page:

Dear Editor,

This is a call to all Bible-believing Christians in Armadillo and throughout Sherman County to take a stand against the evil influences that are invading our community. The Mormons are planning to build a church here, and it is up to us as Christians to stop them. Mormons claim to be Christians, but their claims can't be farther from the truth. The Bible specifically says that there shall be no more books added to it. Look at the last few verses of the book of Revelation and see for yourself. Mormons will try to brainwash you into believing that their Book of Mormon adds to the Bible. However if you are truly a Christian and have read your Bible, you know that's not true. Mormons are a cult and they will tell lies in order to convert you. We must not allow them to build a church in our community. Bring a sign and join me and many other Christians as we hold a protest at their groundbreaking. Stand up for Jesus and stand up for Armadillo!

Sincerely,
Rhanda Mudd

At seminary the next morning Dani had the nerve to ask me if I'd seen the letter.

"Yeah."

"So are you still going to go to the groundbreaking?"

"Of course. Aren't you?"

Dani looked down at her seminary student manual. "Rhanda Mudd is Hunter's cousin."

My blood began to boil. "Why should that matter?"

"Hunter's family doesn't like Mormons."

"Then why are you going out with him?"

Dani shifted in her seat. "I'm hoping to convert him."

I found her reasoning hard to believe. I gripped my LDS scripture marker with both hands. "What makes you think you can convert him?"

"I want to set a good example for him."

The pencil snapped. "By throwing yourself on him? That's some example."

Sister Hooper entered the room and gave us a pop quiz, so I had to stop talking. I filled mine out, turned the papers over, and tried to memorize a scripture mastery while we waited for Dani to finish. She took the whole class period, and even then she was only halfway through the test.

When class was over she followed me out to my truck.

"Do you want a ride to school?"

Dani's eyes were red and glossy. "No."

"Why don't you go to the groundbreaking?" I asked. "If you really want to set an example for Hunter, stand up for the gospel. I'll be there with you. We'll stand together."

"I don't want his family to know I'm Mormon."

I tossed my backpack onto the seat. "I'm going to the groundbreaking. I don't care what other people think of me."

Dani hugged her books to her chest. "I knew you wouldn't understand."

"What's there to understand? Hunter Rockwell's not interested in you. He doesn't care what you think or how you feel. You act so desperate around him—he lets you hang around because he sees that you'll do anything to be his girlfriend."

Dani's cheeks turned bright red. "Listen to Mister High and Mighty. If you're so Christlike, then why are you throwing stones instead of helping me convert Hunter? You're worse than Rhanda Mudd. Sure, Rhanda doesn't like Mormons. But you don't like me unless I'm acting like a Mormon."

"That's not true! I care about you."

Dani's mother pulled up.

A dark shadow fell across Dani's face. "You're a hypocrite." She threw her books in the van, got in, and slammed the door.

I slammed my truck door in response. As Dani left, her cold words lingered in my heart. I zipped my jacket all the way up to my neck and turned the heater on full blast.

I still couldn't get warm.

Chapter Six

The groundbreaking for the Armadillo chapel took place on a cold, gray November afternoon. The anti-Mormon crowd ended up being nothing more than a handful of protesters; they were quiet and didn't cause a scene. They stood on the sidewalk opposite the property and held up signs that said stuff like "Christians Beware" and "Don't Let the Mormons Fool You," with the second *m* crossed out to make the word look like *Morons*. I spotted Rhanda Mudd right away. She was the only one in the crowd who resembled Hunter Rockwell.

Church members outnumbered the protesters, and their spirits were higher, too. The mayor and city council were there, and they applauded when President Carter turned the first shovel of dirt. Dylan and Derek behaved themselves for a change and didn't punch, kick, hit, or bite each other through the entire ceremony from what I could tell. Sister Carter took a picture of her husband holding the golden shovel.

The *Courier* photographer was there too, and the next day President Carter's photograph was on the front page. Dani had avoided the ground-breaking because she didn't want Hunter's family to know she was Mormon. Well, there was her dad's smiling face all over the front page. Hunter's family had to know her secret by now.

Underneath President Carter's photo there was a smaller photo of the missionaries serving in our branch, accompanied by a nice article. Elders Boaz and Tolino talked about their homes and their families and what they were sacrificing to serve their two-year missions. They talked about how much they liked the Armadillo area and how they'd grown to love the people in the community. And each one bore his testimony of Christ.

The Sunday following the groundbreaking, Mom had to speak in sacrament meeting. She sat up on the stand next to Dad. I didn't want to sit by myself, and I sure couldn't sit with Dani. So I sat with the missionaries.

"So, how's the teaching going? Are you guys having any luck?"

Elder Tolino's brow furrowed. "Luck?"

"Yeah. Like, are you having any luck teaching people?"

"Luck doesn't have anything to do with it."

Elder Boaz sighed. "We're doing our best."

Elder Tolino nodded. "No investigators yet, but we're talking to people."

"Maybe the newspaper article will help."

"What newspaper article?" Elder Boaz asked.

"The article about you and Elder Tolino in the *Courier*."

"You mean they printed it?" Elder Tolino looked excited. "Was it good?"

"It was interesting. I didn't know you played college football."

Boaz gave his companion a good-natured punch in the arm. "Tolino's coach begged him not to leave. But he told them he was going no matter what, and they held his scholarship anyway."

"Cool."

And that was the end of that conversation. Or at least I thought so.

That afternoon, Lima Bean and I were enjoying a nap when Mom knocked on the door and woke me up. She cracked the door open and held out the phone. "For you."

Lima Bean yawned, bearing his sharp, white teeth. As he stretched, a funny squeak came from his throat. I rolled off the bed and took the phone.

"Hey."

"Hey, Kevin. This is Elder Boaz. We could use some help."

"What's up?"

"Someone who read the newspaper article about us wants us to tell her more about the Church. We could use a third person."

It was cold outside. The sun was setting. I was groggy. Still . . .

I sighed. "Okay. I'll go."

Thirty minutes later, the missionaries arrived. I got in the backseat and buckled up.

"Where are we going?" I asked as I checked my tie in the rearview mirror.

"539 Palmer Ridge Road," Elder Boaz said. "Let's hope this is a good contact."

The identical cottage-style houses on Palmer Ridge Road were planted in tidy lines along each side of the street. The only way you could tell them apart was by the house numbers and the cars in the driveways. Elder Boaz parked the car along the curb. Elder Tolino said a prayer. Then we went to the front door and knocked.

Rhanda Mudd opened the door and smiled like a cat about to sink her teeth into a mouse. "Come in, gentlemen. I'm so glad you could stop—"

I tapped Elder Tolino on the arm.

"Later," he whispered.

"But you don't know . . ."

It was too late. Boaz had stepped into Rhanda's lair. She motioned for me and Elder Tolino to come in too.

Now I know how a fly feels when it's trapped by a spider, I thought as Rhanda the scheme-weaver welcomed us into her web. We sat down on the couch. It felt sticky.

Rhanda sat across from us. "I read about you boys in the paper. But I didn't read about your friend."

"This is Kevin Kirk," Elder Boaz said. "Sometimes we invite members to help us teach people. We invited him to come with us today."

"Nice to meet you." I tried to sound convincing.

Rhanda sipped her iced tea. "Would you like a drink? Some tea? Or how about a cup of coffee?"

We shook our heads.

"How long have you lived in Armadillo?" Elder Tolino asked.

"I moved here three years ago to take care of my great-aunt. She's ninety-six and isn't able to get out of bed."

Elder Tolino looked at her with genuine admiration. "That's an honorable thing to do."

"It's the *Christian* thing to do," Rhanda replied.

The elders nodded.

"But you wouldn't know what it means to be Christian. That's because Mormons aren't Christians."

I hung my head. *Here we go,* I thought.

"When Christ was dying on the cross, He wanted to make sure someone would take care of His mother after He died," Elder Boaz began, opening his scriptures. "It says in John, chapter nineteen, 'When Jesus therefore saw his mother, and the disciple standing by, whom he loved, he saith unto his mother, Woman, behold thy son! Then saith he to the disciple, Behold thy mother! And from that hour that disciple took her unto his own home.'"

"So you can read the Bible. That doesn't impress me. You do that to lure people in. You convince them you're just like everyone else, that you believe in Jesus, but you don't tell them the truth about your church." Rhanda pointed her finger in Elder Boaz's face. "Then when they're baptized, it's too late."

"We're called to deliver a message to anyone who wants to hear it. We're called to testify that Jesus Christ is the Savior and Redeemer of all people. And we're called to witness that all the scriptures—including the Book of Mormon— are true," Elder Tolino said calmly.

"There you go again, telling me what you think I want to hear—when I know for a fact that your church says the Bible isn't translated correctly." Rhanda picked up her Bible and waved it in the air for emphasis. "The Bible is the one and only word of God. It is the only perfect book in the whole world. Everything, down to the last comma, is perfect. It says at the end of Revelation that there shall be no other books added to the Bible."

Elders Boaz and Tolino stood up. I stood too. It was a relief to be freed from the sticky couch.

Elder Boaz zipped up his scripture case. "We aren't called to argue the message. We're only called to deliver it."

Elder Tolino buttoned his jacket. "We hope we haven't taken too much of your afternoon."

Rhanda laughed. "You can't even defend your own religion. How pathetic. What are you doing out here, anyway? Why don't you go back to Utah?"

"I'm from California," Elder Tolino said. He pointed to Elder Boaz. "He's from Arizona."

Rhanda turned to me. She had bags under her eyes, and I could see that the roots of her hair were darker than the ends. I sensed she was lonely and tired—still, her anger made me uneasy. "You'd better stop hanging around these Mormons. It's not too late for you to get away from their influence. I can help you." She thrust two pamphlets in my hand—"Fifteen Reasons Mormons Aren't Christians" and "How to Leave the Mormons and Find Jesus."

I followed the elders to the door. A weak voice called out from the other room. "Rhanda, I want to meet your visitors."

Annoyed, Rhanda yelled back, "They're leaving, Auntie Belle."

"Let me see them first," Auntie Belle pleaded.

Elder Tolino's hand was on the doorknob. He paused.

Rhanda huffed. "This way." She stomped to the adjoining room where Auntie Belle lay in her hospital bed. The room smelled funny—and I realized why when I saw the adult-size potty chair in the corner.

"They're from some church in town," Rhanda said flatly.

"You look like a nice boy." Auntie Belle reached for my hand. I let her take it. Hers was bony and the veins were pronounced. But she had a strong grip.

Her eyes locked with mine, and I felt a twinge in my chest. *Grandma,* my thoughts whispered. *Her hand feels like Grandma.*

"What's wrong, sweetie?"

Be honest. My thoughts raced. *Be honest.*

"My grandma died a few years ago. You remind me of her."

Auntie Belle's smile was sincere. "You have a pleasant face."

I gave her hand a squeeze. "Thanks."

Elder Boaz spoke up. "We didn't realize there was anyone else home. Thanks for inviting us back here. It's nice to meet you, Auntie Belle."

Auntie Belle let go of my hand. "You boys come back anytime. Rhanda will fix us some supper and we'll have a fun visit. You will come back, won't you?"

"If you want us to, and if it won't trouble your niece," Elder Tolino said.

"I do," Auntie Belle replied. "I don't get a lot of company."

With Rhanda standing beside us, groaning her displeasure, I could see why she didn't have visitors.

Auntie Belle looked hopefully at Rhanda. "You wouldn't mind, would you?"

"Mind what?"

"If these boys come back to see me?"

Rhanda crossed her arms. "If that's what you want."

Auntie Belle clapped. "Then I'll see you soon, won't I? You won't wait too long to come back?"

"We'll be back soon. We promise," Elder Tolino said.

Elder Boaz nodded in agreement.

Auntie Belle looked at me. "You too?"

I grinned. "Me too."

Rhanda was waiting for us at the front door. "In five minutes Auntie Belle won't remember you were here, so don't get your hopes up about coming back. I won't have you comin' over here, preachin' and tryin' to baptize her. Got it?"

The elders acknowledged Rhanda as they walked out the door. I didn't even look at her. But the feel of Auntie Belle's grip lingered on my hand.

As Elder Boaz backed out of the driveway, he smiled at me in the rear mirror. "We'll be back."

Elder Tolino nodded.

"Rhanda just told you not to come back," I said. "She'll have a pit bull waiting for you if you do."

Elder Boaz put the car in drive and took off. "Did you feel it?"

"Sure did," his companion replied.

"The death rays shooting from Rhanda's eyes? Yeah, I felt 'em," I said.

The elders ignored my sarcastic remark.

"The Spirit," Elder Tolino said quietly.

Elder Boaz nodded in agreement.

Chapter Seven

On Thanksgiving Day, Mom, Dad, Granddad, and I cooked the meal at our house and carried it across the street to Marcy's. When we arrived, Marshall took the turkey from Dad.

"Marcy was up and down all night. She's not feeling much better today."

Concern clouded Dad's face. "Maybe we should wait and have Thanksgiving dinner when she's rested."

"No," Marshall insisted. "She wants everyone to be here. She'll be down in a minute. She's been looking forward to dinner. She loves Granddad's turkey dressing."

Lily B wrapped her arms around my leg. "Unka Kebin! Did you bring Lima Bean?"

"No. He has to stay at home."

"Dat's not fair," Lily B pouted. "Cats want to have Fanksgibings too."

"Trust me, Lima Bean doesn't even know it's Thanksgiving."

"He does too, and you left him all alone." Lily B punched me in the thigh. "Go home and get him."

Mom scooped Lily B up. "What's wrong, baby?"

"Can Lima Bean have Fanksgibings wif us, Nana?"

"Of course he can. Kevin, go get the cat."

"But Mom—"

"No buts. Get the cat."

"No buts," Lily B echoed. Then she stuck out her tongue. I tried to snatch it. She pulled it back in.

I went back to get Lima Bean. He was sitting in the kitchen window.

"Come on, buddy." I put him in the pet carrier and took him to Marcy's. When I let him out, he ran to the kitchen window.

Lily B clapped her hands when he successfully landed on the sill. "See, he's happy now. He's wif his fam-ly."

Lima Bean held up his hind leg and licked it all the way up to his paw.

I put Lily B in her booster seat and then sat down in the chair beside her. "Want a drumstick?" I reached across the table and picked up the turkey leg.

Lily B's eyes widened.

"Oh no you don't." Marcy pushed my hand down until the drumstick was back on the platter. "Lily doesn't need that big ol' hunk of turkey. She won't even eat half of what you've put on her plate."

When everyone was seated around the table, Marshall tapped his glass with a spoon. "Let's give thanks. It is Thanksgiving, after all."

I put the spoon back in the bowl of mashed potatoes and folded my hands in my lap.

"Would you bless the food?" Marshall asked Dad.

"I don't mind, but it *is* your home," Dad said.

Marcy elbowed Marshall. "Daddy K's right."

Marshall bowed his head. "Dear God, we are grateful for this holiday. We are grateful that Thy love has made us a family—"

I opened one eye and looked around the table. Mom and Dad were holding hands, their heads bowed close together. Granddad's elbows were on the table, and he rested his chin in his hands. Marcy had one arm around Marshall and the other around her pregnant belly. Lily B was stuffing slices of jellied cranberry sauce into her mouth.

My parents loved Marcy as much as if she were really their daughter. When they told people that Lily B was their granddaughter or that Marshall was their son-in-law, they meant it.

My mom and dad were pretty terrific.

Marshall was right. God's love had made us a family. I closed my eye and listened to the rest of Marshall's prayer.

"Bless us that we will always be mindful of Thy love for us. Amen."

I started to say amen, but a small hand shoved cranberry sauce in my mouth.

"That was a beautiful prayer, sweetheart," Marcy said to Marshall.

"Cramberry face, cramberry face," Lily B chanted.

I swallowed the cranberry sauce. "Silly Lily Billy."

"Silly Unka Kebin." Lily B picked up another slice of cranberry sauce. It slipped and splattered onto her plate.

"Silly both of you," Marcy said. "Lily, sit down and eat your food. Kevin can feed himself."

"Here, have a roll," Granddad said to Lily B. He buttered the roll and set it on her plate.

"Fank you, Gam-pa." Lily B threw him a kiss. Granddad threw one back.

"Well, it's that time," Dad announced as he poured gravy over his dressing and mashed potatoes. "Everyone has to name one thing they're thankful for. If you don't, you have to wash the dishes all by yourself. You go first, Kev."

I wanted to say I was thankful that my parents were color blind. I wanted to say I was thankful that Granddad was living close to us. I wanted to say that I was thankful for Marcy, who was like a big sister to me. I wanted to say I was thankful to have Marshall for a friend. I wanted to say I was thankful for Lily B.

But I didn't say any of that. Instead, I said, "I'm thankful for Lima Bean."

Mom raised her eyebrow. "And?"

"I'm thankful that Granddad made the turkey dressing this year instead of Mom."

"I second your thankfulness for the dressing," Granddad piped up.

Dad nodded, his mouth too full of turkey to add anything to the discussion.

Mom gave him a playful slap on the arm. "Arlice!"

Dad swallowed. "You know your dressing is slimy. You always put oysters in it. I hate slimy dressing." He turned to Lily B. "Now, what is Grandpa's baby thankful for?"

"I'm tankful I'm hafing a baby brudder." Lily B pinched off tiny pieces of her roll and floated them in her gravy.

"What if it's a sister?" Marshall asked.

"Mommy's growing me a brudder," Lily B said matter-of-factly.

"I'm thankful that all the people I love are healthy and happy," Mom said.

Dad wiped the gravy off his moustache with his napkin. "I'm thankful we didn't have to do a funeral today. It's nice to have a normal turkey dinner for a change."

Granddad rested his fork on the edge of his plate. "I'm thankful Sears is having a big sale on tools tomorrow. I plan to make my son go and buy some new ones." He wagged his finger at Dad. "When you were younger I taught you to buy good tools and to take care of them. And what do you do when you're an adult? You buy cheap tools and *still* don't take care of them."

Dad scooped up some more dressing. "I'm thankful my father lives here. I need someone to take care of my tools."

I saw Mom nudge Dad under the table. She tilted her head in Marcy's direction.

Marcy's eyes were fixed on her plate. She was sweating and biting her lip.

"Are you okay?" Dad asked.

Marcy didn't respond.

Marshall massaged her lower back. "Are you sick to your stomach again?"

Marcy gripped the table and shook her head.

Granddad rose from his chair and put his arm around Marcy's shoulders. "Let's walk over to the couch. You look like you need to lie down."

Dad got up too. "We'll get some pillows and put your feet up."

"I'll be all right." Marcy pushed her plate back and scooted away from the table.

Mom got a damp washcloth and patted Marcy's face. "You're sweating like a pig. Are you having contractions?"

"I'm not sure. I just feel . . . strange."

Marshall went for the phone. "I'm calling the doctor."

"Is my little brudder coming?" Lily B asked.

"Mommy's not sure," Marcy replied. She stood up slowly. "Mommy just needs to—"

Then there was a loud splat. Water was spreading all over the floor, and Marcy was standing in the middle of it.

"Your water broke, Marcy. Kevin, run and get a mop." Mom's voice was uncharacteristically calm. She turned to Dad and pointed to Granddad. "You two help her to the bathroom. I'll get some dry clothes and be right there."

"Is this bad?" I whispered to Mom after Dad and Granddad had Marcy in the hall.

"No. It just means that she's going into labor. We need to get her to the hospital." She went to the kitchen, and I could hear her talking to Marshall. "Tell the doctor that Marcy's water broke, and we're leaving for the hospital."

I got the mop and started cleaning things up. Mom ran upstairs to get Marcy's things.

I felt a timid tug on my jeans. "Unka Kebin?" Lily B's dark eyes were swimming in tears. "Is Mommy okay?"

I squatted down and Lily B wrapped her arms around my neck.

I patted her on the back. "It's time for your little brother to be born. Mommy's okay. She's going to the hospital now."

"What about me? Do I have to go too?"

"No. You'll stay here. And while Mommy's gone, I'll stay here and take care of you."

Lily B patted my back in return. "And I'll stay here and take care of Lima Bean."

Lima Bean chirped and leapt from the window. He slinked across the room, jumped on a chair, and sniffed the table.

"Why don't you give Lima Bean some turkey while I finish cleaning up?" I took the slice of white meat off my plate and put it in Lily B's hand. She ran to the den and Lima Bean followed in an easy, expectant trot.

"Where's the keys?" Marshall asked.

I pointed to the counter.

"I'll bring the car around." He snatched up the keys and ran out the door.

Dad and Granddad came in just as I finished mopping. Dad began covering the food. "Looks like our Thanksgiving meal will have to be postponed. We'd better get this in the refrigerator."

Granddad put the aluminum foil back over the sweet potatoes and carried them to the kitchen.

Marcy came in, Mom walking alongside to keep her steady. Dad abandoned the peas and carrots and went to Marcy. He brushed the stray wisps of hair away from her forehead. "Would you like me to give you a father's blessing?"

Marcy's hands were trembling. She sat down.

Marshall ran in. "The car's ready, and I got the suitcase—"

"I want Daddy K to give me a blessing," Marcy said to Marshall.

Marshall looked at Marcy. "Is that what you want?"

She nodded.

Marshall turned to Dad. He didn't say anything. He didn't have to.

Dad placed his hands on Marcy's head. "Marcy Ellen Cartwright, by the power of the Melchezidek priesthood, I pronounce this blessing upon you." His voice was firm and sure, without hesitation or uncertainty. "Angels are attending you and the child that will soon be born. The Lord is mindful of your family and is watching over your daughter and your husband. The Lord wants you to know that He loves you and that He has guided your life in the past, to lead you to people who would love you."

Mom choked back a sob.

"The Lord is aware of the righteous desires of your heart. If you will open your heart to Him, He will help you understand the Book of Mormon and the other scriptures you are reading so that you can gain a testimony of them, and so your righteous desire to have an eternal family can come true."

Marcy was reading the scriptures?

When the blessing was over, Marshall took Marcy's arm. "Are you going to follow?"

"We'll be right behind you," Dad said.

Granddad got the suitcases and left with Marcy and Marshall.

"Will you stay here with Lily?" Mom asked.

"Of course," I replied.

Mom hugged me, then ran across the street to get the car. Lily B curled up on the couch with Lima Bean. She was telling him a story about a girl whose little brother got in trouble for eating all the cramberry sauce at Fanksgibings, but she rescued him by sending the cat to the grocery store to buy more.

Dad and I put the rest of the food away while he waited for Mom to get the car.

"I didn't know Marcy was reading the Book of Mormon," I said.

Dad scraped the food off the last plate and put it in the dishwasher. "I didn't either."

Chapter Eight

Desmond Louis Cartwright was born the day after Thanksgiving. The next afternoon I took Lily B to the hospital. We rode the elevator to the maternity floor. I held Lily B up to the nursery window and pointed to the bassinet that had the "Baby Cartwright" sign on it. Desmond was swaddled in a light blue blanket. All you could see was his face.

"There he is," I said. "That's your little brother."

"Where's his arms and legs?"

"They're bundled up in the blanket."

"Will he like Lima Bean?"

"I'm sure."

"Will Lima Bean like him best?"

"I doubt it. Desmond's too little to play with him yet."

"Good," Lily B said. "I want Lima Bean to like me best."

"C'mon, squirt. Let's go see your mother."

When we found Marcy's room, I let Lily B knock on the door.

"Come in," Marcy sang. Lily B peeked around the door.

"Don't be shy," Marcy called to Lily B.

Lily B turned to me. "I don't want to."

I picked her up and carried her in the room.

Marcy looked ready to cry when she saw Lily B. "Come here, baby." She reached for Lily B, but Lily B turned away and hid her face in my shoulder.

"It's okay," I spoke softly in her ear. "Let your mom hold you."

I sat Lily B down on the bed next to her mother. She put her thumb in her mouth and flopped back onto the pillow.

Marshall brought in a tray from the cafeteria. "Here's your lunch. Two double cheeseburgers, an extra-large order of onion rings, coleslaw, dill pickles, gelatin salad, and three cartons of chocolate milk."

Marcy opened one of the cartons. "Want some chocolate milk, baby?"

Lily B took her thumb out of her mouth. "Gimme a straw, Daddy."

Marshall found a straw and stuck it in the carton. Lily B scooted closer to her mother and slurped her milk.

After I hugged Marcy, I asked, "How are you feeling, besides hungry?"

"Great." She squirted mustard out of a small packet onto the first cheeseburger. "Doctor says I can go home tomorrow."

Marshall helped himself to one of Marcy's onion rings. "I'm going home later to make sure Desmond's room is ready. There are still some baby things in the attic we haven't unpacked."

Lily B's chocolate milk carton was empty. She took the straw out and looked inside.

"Want some more milk?" Marcy asked.

"No, Mommy. But I hafta go to the bafroom." Lily B rolled off the bed and ran to Marshall. "Will you help me, Daddy? I hafta potty."

"Sure thing." Marshall took Lily B's hand. "We'll be right back, Mommy." He took Lily B into the adjoining bathroom and closed the door.

I stepped closer to Marcy's bed. There was a question I was dying to ask her. "Are you reading the Book of Mormon?"

Marcy's eyes widened. "Marshall and I hadn't told anyone about that. I don't know how Daddy K knew. When he said it in the blessing, I almost fell out of the chair."

"What made you start reading it?"

"When I got pregnant with Desmond, Marshall said he thought we should start going to church. He said if we wait until our children are older, they won't want to go. He says we should start now while they're young."

I copied Marshall and nabbed one of Marcy's onion rings.

She continued. "We've gone to a couple of churches in town, but they haven't felt right. It's like there's someplace we're supposed to be and we haven't figured it out yet. Then one day when Marshall and I were talking about it, he remembered something you said to him a few years ago. You told him you knew God had led your family here so we'd find each other. And you said that God meant for families to be together, even in heaven."

I remembered that conversation. "I didn't think Marshall believed me. He acted like I was crazy."

"Guess you were wrong, little brother." Marcy grinned. "Marshall said he wanted to learn more about your church. I thought it would be best not to tell anyone. If we decide not to join, I don't want to hurt Momma and Daddy K."

The toilet flushed.

"Don't say anything, okay?" Marcy whispered. "I don't understand a lot of what we're reading, and we're still trying to decide what to do."

"I'll keep it quiet."

Marshall opened the bathroom door. Lily B bounced out. "Let's go see Desmond, Daddy. Can Mommy go too?"

Marcy sat up and put on her robe. "Get my slippers, Kevin."

I handed Marcy her purple knit slippers. As we walked to the visiting area, I wondered how I could convince Marcy and Marshall that coming to our church would be the right thing to do. But every idea that crossed my mind seemed pushy or trite. I didn't know how to help them.

If I didn't know how to help my own sister understand the gospel, I sure wouldn't be able to help anyone else. And if I didn't have the skills to be a missionary, then there wasn't much reason for me to be one, was there?

After we were seated, a nurse entered the room carrying Desmond. The nurse sat down beside Lily B and placed Desmond in her arms. Lily B's eyes were bright and round with delight. "Lookit me, Mommy! I can hold Desmond! And he's not crying!"

Marcy and Marshall cooed over Desmond and praised Lily B for being such a good big sister.

"I will tell you about Lima Bean. He's Unka Kebin's cat, but Lima Bean likes me best," Lily B whispered to Desmond. "If you gib him your food he'll like you, too—but he'll still like me best 'cause I was first."

The next morning I went out to do some sketches in my wildlife journal. When I finished, I filled out the application for Nelson-Barrett U, put it in the postage-paid envelope, and put it in the mailbox.

If I wasn't going on a mission, then I needed to start making plans for college.

* * *

Not long after Desmond was born, President Carter caught me after church. "I'd like to speak to you, Kevin."

"Will it take long?"

"No." He opened the door to his makeshift office. "Have a seat." I sat down in the beat-up wooden chair. "I hear you're eighteen now. Congratulations."

"Thanks."

"Once you graduate from high school, you can be ordained an elder in the Melchizedek priesthood." Then President Carter crossed his arms and stared at the painting of Jesus on the wall and didn't say anything for what seemed like fifteen minutes. The long silence was awkward. I decided to ask him about Dani. I hadn't seen her at church for a couple of Sundays.

"Is Dani sick today?"

"No."

Silence again.

"I guess I'll see her in seminary tomorrow."

President Carter rubbed the back of his neck as if his muscles were tense and needed to be loosened. "Dani is struggling. Do me a favor—don't stop being her friend. She needs you right now. You're the only person her age in the Church."

"I've tried. But she left me at homecoming, remember?"

"I remember."

"I don't think she wants to be friends with me anymore."

"Maybe she doesn't." He wrung his hands. "To be honest, I don't know what to do. I'm running out of options. I'm praying for more." He cleared his throat, then sat up straight and opened a folder that was lying on his desk. "But that's not why I asked you here. The time has come for you to decide if you will serve a mission. My job is to help you during the next few months as you prepare to make that decision. Have you given this any thought?"

I didn't feel comfortable saying what was on my mind. How could I be a missionary if I didn't know how to convince someone the Church is true? I didn't know how to convince Marcy and

Marshall. I didn't know how to convince Rhanda Mudd. And I sure didn't know how to convince Dani. Besides, I'd sent in my application to Nelson-Barrett U. "Dad told me once that he'd like for me to. But he also said it had to be my decision, not his."

"Your father's right. No one can—or should— make that choice for you. This is between you and the Lord. But as long as you're healthy and there are no extenuating circumstances, you need to prayerfully consider it." He took a folder out of his desk drawer and handed it to me. "This is the application. It's not time to fill it out now. You should read over it and become familiar with it. There's more to serving a mission than spiritual preparation. You'll have to have a physical, get any necessary dental work completed, make financial arrangements—"

"What about college? What if I get a scholarship? Two years is a long time to be away from college."

President Carter scratched his chin. "Have you read the Book of Mormon?"

"Sure."

"I mean, have you read it—first page to last."

I felt the red creep up my cheeks.

President Carter leaned back in his chair. It squeaked, and the sound of metal scraping against metal made my jaw hurt. "I want you to read the Book of Mormon all the way through. Will you do that? We'll talk again when you've finished. Can you have it read by, say, the end of March?"

I thought about all the homework I had to do, my seminary assignments, and my chores at the Paramount. I barely had time to write in my wildlife journals. Now, on top of all that, I had four months to read the Book of Mormon.

"I'll try," I said. But I wasn't too enthused.

"Good." President Carter stood up and walked with me to the door. "Remember what I told you about Dani. Be her friend."

"I haven't stopped."

He shook my hand. His grip was tight, almost desperate. "Please don't."

Chapter Nine

Dani's parents wouldn't let her drive the mini-van on weekends unless she attended seminary during the week. So in December she didn't miss a single day. She even started riding with me to school again.

One morning, a few days before midterms and the holiday break, she asked me if I was going to the Holly Berry Ball, the school's annual night-before-New-Year's-Eve dance.

Of course I'd heard of it, but I acted like I hadn't.

"I hope I get to go," Dani said. "I just need someone to ask me."

It occurred to me that she wanted me to take the hint and ask her. Her father's words echoed in my ears: *Be her friend.* But I hadn't forgotten homecoming night and how she'd dumped me the minute she had a chance to get to Hunter Rockwell.

So I didn't ask, and Dani looked disappointed when I parked the truck in the school lot and got

out without so much as a hint of an offer. I didn't
care if she was asked to the Holly Berry Ball or
not. I had more important stuff on my mind.

First, I had the commitment I'd made to
President Carter to read the Book of Mormon.
I'd read the title page—that was it. He wanted
me to think about serving a mission. But I'd
received a packet full of scholarship applications
for Nelson-Barrett U, along with an application
for their undergrad research program, and it was
hard to think about anything else. Dr. Wallace
had been true to his word and had nominated
me for a full scholarship! I'd been studying for
midterms; we'd had a body at the Paramount
every night since the first of December, and I'd
been helping my parents with visitations every
day after school. I even had to miss church one
Sunday to help Mom with a funeral.

It was a relief when midterms were over. I
planned to get up every morning at seven during
the break and get caught up on my wildlife journals. But the first morning of winter break Dad
woke me up at six. He had to pick up a body in
Paducah, Kentucky. The trip there and back
would take most of the day. Mom needed
Marshall to help her get ready for the evening's
visitation, Marcy had her hands full with little
Des, and Granddad was having a root canal.

Dad was left with two choices: take me or take the cat. Somehow Lima Bean avoided the draft. I put on a suit and tie.

The monotonous rhythm of the interstate drive lulled me back to sleep. I woke up when Dad stopped to gas up at a convenience store in Blytheville. Dad gave me a ten and told me to go in and get breakfast. I got a pork chop biscuit, a Yoo-hoo, and a Hunk-O-Choklit bar with extra nuts. I got Dad two egg and cheese biscuits, two cans of diet soda, and three crème-filled donuts.

Once we were back on the interstate, Dad put in an Elvis CD and cranked up the volume. When his mouth wasn't full of biscuits and donuts, he sang along with the King. I ate my biscuit and candy bar quietly. When I was finished, there was nothing else to do but stare out the window at the flat landscape.

As Elvis sang "I Got Stung," we crossed over from Arkansas into the Missouri boot heel. By the time Elvis sang the last note of the last song on the CD, we were at the Sikeston exit. Dad stopped at another convenience store, and I filled up the hearse while he went to the restroom.

Dad put in another Elvis CD, and we got back on the interstate. Several tunes later, Dad was harmonizing with Elvis on "I Forgot to

Remember to Forget" when he whizzed past our turnoff.

I shook Dad's shoulder. "We were supposed to go that way."

"I know."

"Then why'd you pass the exit?"

Dad turned Elvis off in the middle of "Steamroller Blues."

"I want to show you something," he said.

Dad *never* turned Elvis off in the middle of a song.

Soon we were crossing the Mississippi River. Halfway over the bridge a sign welcomed us to Illinois. "I'm not seeing anything yet," I said.

"You will."

Since Dad obviously didn't need my map-reading skills, I decided to fold the map and put it in the glove compartment. But maps never fold up to look the same once you've unfolded them. I fought with the paper until I was ready to wad it and throw it into the river.

Finally, Dad interrupted my map wrestling. "Here we are—Fort Defiance." He parked the hearse, and we walked to what looked like a miniature concrete boat ramp. We stood at the edge; the river lapped close to our feet. I stuck my hands in my pockets and stared out at the water.

Dad nudged me. "Do you realize where we are?"

"At the river?"

"That's the Ohio River," he pointed to the left, "and the Mississippi is to the right. We're standing at the confluence of two of the mightiest rivers in America. Here the two become one." He opened his arms in a futile attempt to embrace the enormous view. "This is awesome stuff."

"So we're standing at the tip of Illinois."

"You know your geography. There's Kentucky," he pointed to the left, then to the right, "and Missouri."

The waters of the Ohio were greenish; the Mississippi's, brown. I stepped to the edge of the concrete ramp and dipped my hand in the water. My arm tingled.

I grinned at Dad. There were a lot of things I wanted to say, but none of them were things I wanted to say out loud. So I settled for a one-word exclamation. "Cool."

"It's more than cool. It's—it's magical. At least to me." Dad squatted beside me and put his hand in the water too. "You can feel the history, the energy this place has. There are ancient Indian mounds in this area. Lewis and Clark stopped here. Civil War generals fought for control of this confluence. Mark Twain was inspired by it."

The wind picked up. I was cold, but I didn't want to leave. I had never stood at the edge of anything that was so much bigger than me. *This must be how astronauts feel when they look out from the space shuttle and see the earth,* I thought. I'd never felt so small. And I didn't know that feeling small could make me feel so good.

"It took me a long time, Kevin, but I think I've finally got things figured out. And it has to do with this spot."

"What do you mean?"

"I sat on the bank too long." Dad gazed out on the river as if he were trying to bring the end into focus. "I let too much time flow by." He dried his hand with his handkerchief and then handed it to me so I could do the same.

"I don't understand."

Dad continued. "I ignored my testimony for a long time." Dad stuck his hands in his pockets and jingled his keys. "When God saw I was ignoring the truth, He sent a flood that forced me into the river. I tried to swim against it, tried to get back to my comfortable spot on the bank, but the current was too strong. I couldn't fight my testimony. I had to come back to church."

"There have been times I wished I could crawl back to that comfortable spot on the bank," he went on, "times I wanted to escape the responsibility of *knowing* the truth. But you can't ignore the power of the river. You can't fight the truth. The truth is bigger than you and me—bigger than anything."

I breathed in the deep, moist air.

"I feel very small standing here, Kevin."

I'd been taller than Dad for years. But as we stood at the confluence and I listened to him bear his testimony, I realized I needed to measure his height with something more appropriate than a yardstick.

"Can I tell you something, Dad?"

"Sure."

I choked down the lump in my throat. "You're the biggest guy I know."

A barge entered from the Ohio. We waved and the captain blew the horn.

Dad checked his watch. "We need to go."

We got back in the hearse and drove to Paducah.

It was late in the afternoon when we headed back to Armadillo. We crossed the Ohio River, this time with a dead body in tow. The bridge that spanned the Mississippi was a short distance away. We'd have to cross it, too, to get back home.

As we drove over the second bridge, I watched the mighty Mississippi embrace its companion, and together they rolled on toward the Gulf of Mexico, their blended currents glazed by the sweetness of the sunset.

* * *

The Sunday before Christmas, Dani hounded me about the Holly Berry Ball during the whole forty-five minutes of Sunday School and Sister Hooper's lesson about the seven seals in the book of Revelation. Then she followed me to priesthood, yapping on about how she knew she could borrow a dress from her friend Lisa, a new girl in her stats class.

"Look, I gotta go. Brother Conrad's saving me a seat in priesthood meeting."

Dani grabbed my arm in a show of unusual force. "I really want to go to the Holly Berry Ball. Will you go with me?"

"Why are you so desperate?" I jerked myself out of her grip. "It's just a dumb ol' dance."

"*Everyone's* going to be there. I'll be the only girl in the senior class who's not." Her brown eyes gazed into mine, and for a second I felt like a large-mouth bass the moment before he bites down on a lure. Fortunately I saw the sharp, polished hook and backed away just in time.

"I haven't forgotten the last time I took you to a dance."

Dani's face turned red—not from embarrassment, but anger. "I have to go to this dance. Especially since Hunter asked—"

"Aha! The truth comes out. Hunter didn't ask you!"

She hung her head. "He asked me."

My chest cramped with envy. "Don't go out on a date with him."

"My parents won't let me. I had to tell him no."

"Then what's the problem?"

"Everyone knows he's asked me out. I'll look stupid if I don't go. I told him that I already had another date. That's why I need you to take me."

"Why do you care what other people think?"

"You'd understand if you were in my shoes."

I couldn't believe we were having this conversation. "Remember back in seventh grade when I first moved to Armadillo? When I was having trouble with Chuck Stiller? Remember how he hounded me every day, how he wanted to beat me up? What did you say? You said don't do something out of pride you'll regret later. Don't do something you'll wish you hadn't done."

"But this is different."

"No it's not."

A tear spilled over her lashes and down her cheek, leaving behind a streak of makeup. "Thanks for caring."

She passed her father, President Carter, as she walked away from me. She gave him a big fake smile as if everything was fine.

Hunter Rockwell—Mister Sherman County Football, Best Dressed, Biggest Flirt, Most Likely to Get His Way—was a jerk. If his influence could sway Dani from listening to me, her parents, and all the people who loved her—well, Hunter was a bigger jerk than I'd thought.

Then it occurred to me. Was Dani's behavior really Hunter's fault? She knew the difference between right and wrong, after all.

Dani didn't say anything else about the dance, so I figured she didn't go. But after the holiday break, wherever I saw Dani, I saw Hunter. And surprisingly, when I saw Dani she was friendly—more so than I'd expected, considering I'd refused to take her to the dance.

Then I saw the picture.

I was sitting in senior English. We had a sub that day, and since everyone had completed the day's assignment, he let us have free time. Tiff Beeny and Jillian Wheeler, the senior class gossip queens, were going through their collection of couples' photos from the Holly Berry Ball and compiling a best/worst dressed list. They were making up their own set of juvenile awards with categories like cutest couple, most expensive corsage, or girl with the heaviest makeup.

Tiff snickered. "Look at Tara and Michael. They look like they bought their outfits at a funeral home."

Why are stupid conversations always louder than conversations worth listening to?

"Now *there* is the luckiest girl at the dance," Jillian said as she handed Tiff another photo. "She gets the award for biggest catch."

"It's not fair, Jilly," Tiff whined. "She's so . . ."

"Plain?"

Tiff giggled.

Jillian lowered her voice. "Her dress looks awful."

"It doesn't fit right."

"Even Hunt said she looked bad," Jillian hissed. "Robert told me that he heard from Matt—you know, Matt knows the best friend of the guy who's the trainer for the team—that Hunt was making bets on how long it would take her to have a wardrobe malfunction."

I couldn't wait to tell Dani what I'd heard. She'd be glad that she didn't go to the dance with Hunter. I decided she deserved something special for upholding her standards. Maybe she'd go out with me to the Cow Palace? We could go bowling afterward too.

Tiff chuckled. "She used to make a big deal about her Mormon standards, that she didn't do this or that. Now that she likes Hunter, her standards don't mean so much anymore. Makes you wonder what she's doing to get him to go out with her."

Jillian gave Tiff a knowing look. "He'll get tired of Dani. Then he'll go somewhere else. He always does." She leaned toward Jillian. "I heard he's after that new girl, Lisa."

I gasped.

Tiff and Jillian turned around.

I faked a cough. "Swallowed my gum," I croaked. "Excuse me."

Jillian made a face. "We're not supposed to chew gum in class."

I made a face back. "We're not supposed to be gossiping, either."

"Whatever," Tiff said. She turned to Jillian. "Let's get a restroom pass. See who's out in the hall."

While they were gone I searched through the photos on Tiff's desk. There they were—Dani and Hunter—standing in front of a fake holly bush, and the words *Holly Berry Ball* sparkling above their heads. Hunter was wearing a black tux with a white carnation on the lapel. And Dani . . .

Where the heck did she get that dress? It was long, blue, and sleeveless. It was also neck-less, back-less, and practically chest-less.

Dani had helped me to learn a higher standard. Now she'd lowered hers—just to be accepted. I would have never asked her to change for me. I knew her well enough to know that she was not comfortable in that dress.

When school let out, I ran to her locker, hoping to catch her before she went out to meet her mom in the parking lot.

"Dani, we need to talk."

She ignored me and continued talking to the girls standing around her.

I put my hand on her arm. "Please?"

She turned to the other girls and rolled her eyes. "I have to go. Call me tonight and fill me in on the plans for the weekend."

I heard one girl whisper, "Make sure she doesn't invite *him*."

I knew they were talking about me.

We stopped at the end of the hall. I searched her doe-like eyes. "You went to the Holly Berry Ball, didn't you?"

"So?"

"Your mom and dad let you go?"

She fidgeted. "Please don't tell Mom and Dad! They'll have a fit."

"Why'd you do it?"

"I had to, Kevin. It was *expected*."

"That's a crock."

"My friends are different. You don't understand them."

"I'm your friend, and I would have never asked you to wear that dress to the dance."

Dani's hopeful expression unnerved me. "Did you like it?"

I wanted to tell her how Tiff and Jillian were making fun of her dress. But I didn't. "There's no way your dad would've let you out of the house if he'd seen it."

"I borrowed it from Lisa," Dani said smugly. "I spent the night at her house. Our dates picked us up there."

"People are saying your 'Mormon standards' aren't as important to you anymore."

Dani looked indignant. "I still keep my standards. I don't drink. Ask anybody. I've turned down beer at parties, and my friends are okay with that. I just tell them if they want to drink, I'll be the designated driver."

I couldn't believe what I was hearing. "I never thought you'd go to a keg party."

"You're still mad because you think I dumped you at homecoming. You need to get over that. That was months ago."

I didn't want to tell her. I didn't want to hurt her. But at the same time, part of me wanted the satisfaction of proving to her that she was oh so wrong about her so-called friends.

"So you're not drinking with your friends. That's not the only standard your friends are talking about."

"What do you mean?"

"They're talking about what you've done to make Hunter want to go out with you."

Dani almost dropped her books. Her bottom lip quivered. "I haven't *done* anything." Her face paled, and she held her books close to her stomach as if she was about to throw up.

I walked her out the door and past the line of cars to the parking lot. "I didn't want to hurt you, but you need to know. Don't you see? They're not your real friends. You don't have to be seen with Tiff or Jillian or even Hunter Rockwell for me to think you're an amazing person. You don't have to wear a strapless dress you borrowed from someone else to impress me."

Dani brushed her hair back behind her ear. A glint of silver caught my eye. "What is that?"

"Oh, it's not a real piercing." Dani flipped her hair back over her ear to cover the silver hoop. "Dad would have a stroke if I pierced the top of my ear. I just wear it when I'm at school or out with my friends."

Sister Carter's Buick pulled around the corner. Dani squeezed my arm, pretending to be bright and happy. But I knew she was faking it because her mom was watching. "We'll talk later."

As I watched her drive away, I thought about what Dad had said to me at the confluence of the rivers—how you can only sit on the bank so long before the flood comes along and forces you into the water.

If anyone needed a flood right now, it was Dani.

Chapter Ten

I hadn't been out with the missionaries since the Sunday we went to Rhanda Mudd's. Since that time Elder Boaz had finished his mission. He returned to Arizona shortly after Christmas. Elder Tolino now had an enthusiastic new companion—Elder McDonnell from Alberta, Canada.

One Sunday Elder McDonnell approached me. "Will you go with us to visit an investigator this afternoon?"

"I have other plans." I was way behind on the Book of Mormon reading I'd promised President Carter. It was mid-February, and I hadn't even finished Jacob yet. I still held out hope that a couple of Sabbath-day reading marathons would take care of it.

Elder McDonnell was disappointed. "She was hoping to see you again."

"I don't know any of your investigators."

"She knows you."

"Who?"

"Belle Mudd. We've been visiting her every Sunday since the first of the year. She keeps asking for 'that boy who visited her the first time.' Elder Tolino and I didn't know what she meant. At first we thought she was talking about Elder Boaz. But last week her great-niece told us it was the boy who said she reminded him of his grandmother. Then Elder Tolino realized it was you."

Now that I knew who it was, I really didn't want to go. I wasn't in the mood to deal with Rhanda Mudd. "Listen, I'd like to, but I just can't . . ."

I hesitated, and Elder McDonnell's expression turned hopeful.

The scriptures I carried suddenly weighed fifty pounds. I sighed. "All right."

"We'll see you at three." Elder McDonnell ran to tell Elder Tolino the good news.

That afternoon I fixed a tuna sandwich and a plateful of chips and went to sulk on the couch.

Mom sat down beside me. "Why are you still in your suit?"

"I have to go out with the elders at three." I took a bite of my sandwich.

"What's wrong with that?"

"The woman we're visiting doesn't like Mormons."

"Then why go there?"

"The woman's great-aunt wants to see us."

"How old is she?"

I took another bite, and this time spoke with my mouth full. "Old as dirt."

Mom frowned. "That's not nice. And don't talk with food in your mouth."

I swallowed. "Her nineties. She can't get out of bed."

"The poor thing." Mom got a basket from the closet. She rummaged through the cabinet and found a couple of unused word-find puzzle books. She put them in the basket, along with a pack of new pens, a sack of lemon drops, a trial-size bottle of hand lotion, and several packages of toasted peanut butter crackers. She set the basket in my lap. "I have some pretty ribbon. I'll put a bow on here, and you can tell her this is a sunshine basket—a gift to her from your family."

I ate my sandwich and chips and watched Mom wrestle with the ribbon. Frustrated by her failed attempts at bow making, she tied it to the handle in a shoelace-type knot.

"There," she said, fluffing out the two loops to make them look fuller. "That's not bad."

"No, I guess not."

I heard Dad's footsteps outside. Mom abandoned the basket and ran to the door.

"Are you hungry, sweetie?"

Dad kissed her cheek and took off his suit coat. "What've we got?"

"Tuna."

"Sure." Dad loosened his tie. "Why is Kevin holding that basket? It's not Easter yet."

"He's going out with the missionaries," Mom said proudly. "I'm sending a goody basket for the elderly lady he's visiting."

Dad gave me a thumbs-up.

I shook my head. "No, Dad. This isn't a thumbs-up. This woman lives with her niece who's as anti-Mormon as you can get."

"You never know, son. You might just say something that will change her mind. Besides, doesn't the elderly woman have a right to see the missionaries if she wants?"

I heard a car horn. It was three o'clock. I grabbed the basket and made my way down the steps to the missionaries' car.

"Greetings," Elder Tolino said from the driver's seat.

"Greetings," echoed Elder McDonnell. "What's with the basket?"

"My mom made it for Auntie Belle," I said as I buckled my seat belt.

When we got to Rhanda's house, Hunter's SUV was in the driveway.

"Look guys, I can't go in there. Just take the basket in and give my regrets." I could walk home. It was only fifteen miles to the Paramount.

Elder McDonnell dragged me down the sidewalk. "Auntie Belle wants to see you. We told her you were coming. We called her this afternoon."

Elder Tolino rang the doorbell.

Rhanda Mudd opened the door and allowed the elders to step inside. She looked at me as if I were the Creature from the Black Lagoon. "Where did you come from?"

"Um . . . your great-aunt said she wanted to see me."

Rhanda rolled her eyes and sighed. She nodded toward Auntie Belle's room, and I followed the missionaries.

From the next room, I heard Hunter ask his cousin who was at the door.

"Those crazy Mormons," Rhanda replied.

"You should tell them to go away," a familiar voice interjected. "I'm sure if they know they're not wanted, they'll leave you alone."

"Can't do that," Rhanda said. I heard the click of a cigarette lighter next, then a pause. I figured Rhanda was inhaling. "Auntie Belle wants them to visit. Nobody else comes to see her."

"If you don't want them here, just tell them."

I recognized the voice. My heart stopped for a moment of silence before it shattered.

It was Dani.

I must have stalled, because Elder Tolino nudged me forward. Auntie Belle was asleep. The shades were pulled, making the room depressingly dark.

"Auntie." Elder Tolino nudged the old woman's shoulder. "It's Elder Tolino."

Auntie Belle's eyes barely opened.

"And me, Elder McDonnell," the other missionary said.

Auntie Belle licked her lips. "The other boy— the one who came first—did he come like you promised?"

I gave Elder McDonnell the sunshine basket and stepped forward so Auntie Belle could see me.

"It *is* you! I was so afraid you wouldn't come to see me again."

I took her hand. "I didn't know you wanted to see me."

She put her hand on top of mine. "I was hoping you'd come back, sweetie."

When Auntie Belle said sweetie, it was as if I heard Grandma calling me sweetie again.

I put my other hand over hers. "I'm glad I'm here."

"Oh—you've only got three fingers on your hand." Auntie Belle brought my right hand to her face to examine it closer. "What happened? Were you born that way?"

I pulled my hand away, embarrassed that she'd brought it up. "I lost it in an accident."

"Well, sweetie, I know how you feel." She reached down and uncovered her feet. "I've had some toes amputated. Diabetes done it to me."

Elder McDonnell set Mom's basket on the bed.

"My mom sent you this," I said. "I hope you like it."

Auntie Belle's eyes grew wide. "Oh my—a basket of goodies. Such a pretty bow, too." She fingered Mom's feeble attempt at art. "I don't get many gifts. Please give my appreciation to your mother."

Elder McDonnell opened the curtains. The sun poured in, lifting the mood in the room. Elder Tolino pulled a chair up to the bed. "Did you read this week's assignment?"

"I've read all of Third Nephi," Auntie Bell said, pronouncing the name Neff-ee instead of Nee-fi. Then she giggled. "I have to read at night after Rhanda goes to bed. If she caught me reading the Book of Mormon, she'd never let you come back. I have a flashlight." She giggled as she lifted the corner of her pillow. "I feel like a child, reading at night so my parents won't see."

"Do you have any questions about the reading?" Elder McDonnell asked.

While the elders talked to Auntie Belle, I strained to hear the conversation down the hall. I heard Hunter's deep voice and Rhanda's whiny one. Once in a while the soft lilt of Dani's voice—sounding much like her mother's—interrupted the other two.

I excused myself and went to the front room. I wanted Dani to know I was there. I wanted to make her acknowledge my presence.

Rhanda was seated on the couch, smoking a cigarette. Dani and Hunter sat on the loveseat opposite.

I knocked on the door frame. "Excuse me, Rhanda. I hope I'm not interrupting something. I just want to thank you for allowing us to visit your aunt."

Dani almost dropped her soda.

Rhanda thumped the ashes from the end of her cigarette into an empty soda can. "I guess I should be glad you Mormons come and talk to her. It gives me a break. Just don't get any ideas. You won't baptize either one of us. I know the truth about your church. It's a cult."

Hunter flipped through a worn issue of *Guns and Ammo*. "I'm sure they won't stay long."

Dani sat, petrified. In fact, she wouldn't even look at me.

It irritated Rhanda that I was still in the doorway. "Did you need something else?"

I was going to go back to Auntie Belle's room, but before I turned around I changed my mind. Dani was going to speak to me whether she wanted to or not.

"Hey Dani, do you need a ride to seminary in the morning?"

She was wearing that silver hoop that made it look like she had a piercing on the top part of her ear. She flipped her hair over it and glared at me. "Of course not."

Rhanda's eyes narrowed. She turned to Dani. "What's seminary?"

"A boring church class." Dani rolled her eyes. "I don't know why he's asking me—I only go when I have to."

"Did you know Dani's dad is the branch president at our church?" I volunteered. "He's like our minister. His picture was on the front page of the *Courier* when we had the ground-breaking for our new building."

The silence that followed felt like hours. When Rhanda broke it, I found myself wishing the silence could have lasted forever.

"I know who her daddy is," Rhanda said smugly. She inhaled, held it, and then blew out the smoke in a slow, thin stream. She turned to Dani and smiled affectionately. "I think Dani's old enough to make her own choices about religion. Just because her daddy's a Mormon doesn't mean she has to make the same mistake."

"I know why Dani goes to church," I said. "I know how she feels about it."

Rhanda raised her eyebrows. Dani glanced sideways at Hunter, then lowered her head. "Kevin doesn't know what he's talking about. I go to church because my parents make me." Her shoulders slumped and a dark shadow crossed her face. "I only go because I have to."

Chapter Eleven

March arrived, and I still hadn't finished reading the Book of Mormon. I was in Alma, which is about five hundred chapters long. I didn't want to tell President Carter I'd procrastinated, so on the first Sunday I tried to avoid him. When I saw him coming my direction, I found reasons to turn the other way—everything from helping Sister Conrad set up chairs for Relief Society to helping Sister Carter usher Dani's little brothers to Primary. I felt guilty. If I didn't get serious about my commitment to finish the Book of Mormon, I'd be as old as the General Authorities before I ever made up my mind about a mission.

When we were halfway into March, I realized time was running out. I decided to lock myself in my room until I finished Alma. It was a long Sunday afternoon, especially since Lima Bean chose that time to use his litter box, and the smell was so bad I had to hold my breath. But I knew if I didn't stick with the reading, I'd get sidetracked. I opened my window and sprayed some air freshener in the room. It got rid of the smell, but it insulted my cat. Lima Bean sniffed, and then offered an indignant flick of his tail. He settled in the window seat and watched the redbirds congregating around the feeder in the back lot.

The following Monday as I drove home from school, I cooked up a plan to get in even more reading. I'd ask Mom if we could make that night's home evening a quiet scripture-reading night. Mom would be thrilled that I offered a suggestion for home evening, and I'd get some extra reading done. If I read fast enough, I could even finish Helaman.

I parked the truck in the hearse garage and as I walked to the Paramount, the mail carrier drove up and handed me the mail—including a thick envelope that I had to sign for.

I took the mail upstairs, dumped it on the kitchen table, and sorted it into stacks: Paramount bills, home bills, junk mail, and Granddad's mail. The thick envelope was for me. It was made from a fancy grade of paper and it had a Tennessee return address. Inside there was a blue folder with an impressive gold seal on the front that said *Nelson-Barrett University.*

I eased the elegant cover letter from the folder and began to read.

Dear Kevin:

We are pleased to inform you that you have been chosen to receive a full four-year scholarship to attend Nelson-Barrett University. In addition, your excellent academic record has earned you the opportunity to join the Advanced Undergraduate Research Program, which is a part of our nationally ranked College of Biology and Life Sciences.

We congratulate you on this achievement. Over three hundred highly qualified students applied for this scholarship program, and while it was difficult for the faculty to select the three finalists, you can be assured that your qualifications clearly met the criteria for entry into this prestigious program.

Your acceptance into this program entitles you to four years paid tuition at Nelson-Barrett University, plus qualifies you for additional grants to cover housing, books, and other required fees.

An advisor has been assigned to you. His contact information is at the bottom of this letter. Please complete the enclosed paperwork and return it to him as soon as possible. Once you have notified us that you plan to accept this award, we can begin the process of enrolling you in our school. Again, we congratulate you and look forward to seeing you on campus.

Sincerely,
Ma'shal Rashad
President, Nelson-Barrett University
CC: Dr. Alfred L. Wallace

I jumped on the sofa and used it for a trampoline. Then I ran through the house, beating my chest like a baboon.

"I am the MAN, Lima Bean!"

Lima Bean continued grooming his right leg as if I weren't even in the room.

I went downstairs to tell Mom and Dad, but they weren't there. The office was locked. The guest kitchen was empty.

Maybe they were at Granddad's. I ran across the parking lot and up the stairs to the apartment above the hearse garage. I beat on the door. No answer.

I sprinted to Marcy's. Her door wasn't locked.

"Are you home?" I hollered.

"Come on in," she yelled back.

She was on the floor, changing Desmond's diaper. Lily B was sitting at a child-size table scribbling in her coloring book.

"Unka Kebin!" She waved her coloring book at me. "Will you color wif me?"

"I have some big news. Look what I got." I waved the folder over my head. "A scholarship!"

Marcy clapped her hands. "Is it for the undergrad research program?"

"Yes!" I thrust my arms up in the air like Rocky Balboa and danced around the room.

Marcy finished changing Desmond and put him in his playpen. "I'm so happy for you." She hugged me and kissed my cheek.

"I want to tell Mom and Dad. Where'd they go?"

"They've gone to the Piggly-Wiggly."

"What about Granddad?"

"He had to go back to the dentist. His crown broke."

"Want to see the letter?"

Marcy opened the folder and read the letter. "This is incredible. A full scholarship! I'm impressed." She handed the folder back to me. "I always knew you were smart."

I never even got around to suggesting the scripture reading to Mom. I was too excited about my award. I managed to wait until after supper. We sat down to have home evening and after Mom said the prayer, I whipped out the folder. "I have an announcement. Dad, you wanna read it?"

Dad scanned the letter. He gaped at me in awe. "You won a full scholarship? A four-year scholarship?"

Mom gasped. "Is this true?"

I nodded so hard I thought my head would fall off my neck.

Dad jumped up and grabbed me in a bear hug. "This is fantastic!"

Mom clapped her hands. "A full scholarship. I'm so impressed!" Then she looked at Dad. "I wonder if they'll hold it while—"

I already knew what she was going to say. "I can't turn down a full scholarship to serve a mission."

Dad's smile drooped. Mom suddenly looked somber.

"This is a great achievement." He put the folder back in the envelope. His voice was more subdued. "I'm very proud of you."

"I am too," Mom added, though she didn't seem to be as happy as she was ten seconds ago.

"What's wrong with everybody?" I couldn't believe my parents were acting this way. "Think of all the money you'll be saving. Tuition at Nelson-Barrett U is expensive."

"It's not the tuition," Dad said. "And we *are* proud of you. You worked hard. You earned that scholarship."

"Then what?" I looked at my parents, and all at once it hit me. "Listen. If the Lord wanted me to serve a mission, He wouldn't have dropped this scholarship in my lap."

"Just promise me you'll pray about it before you make a decision," Dad said. "That's all I ask."

"Of course I will," I answered. But there wasn't any need to pray, not when I'd just had tens of thousands of dollars handed to me in a blue folder with a gold seal.

* * *

Granddad liked to say that if you look a gift horse in the mouth long enough, you're gonna find he has some bad teeth. But I couldn't see anything bad about receiving a scholarship. The Lord wouldn't give me something so wonderful only to take it all away. I was sure of it.

Confident I'd made the right decision about my future, I concentrated on meeting my commitment to President Carter. I tripled up on my scripture study, and by the end of March I'd honed my speed-reading skills and finished the Book of Mormon. I went to church the last Sunday of the month ready to face my branch president.

"I finished the reading assignment," I said as I sat down in the chair in front of his desk. "It took me a little longer than I expected, but I finished the Book of Mormon."

I could tell President Carter was pleased. "This was your first time to read it through, right?"

"Yes."

"How did you feel about it?"

"I didn't see any heavenly messengers when I finished. I didn't have any big impressions. I just feel like the scriptures are right."

"May I ask a question?"

"Sure."

President Carter looked me dead in the eye. "Did you read it to satisfy me or to satisfy yourself?"

Darn. I had to be honest. "I promised you I'd read it, so I did."

I sensed he was trying hard to hide his disappointment. "That's commendable. When you decide to read it for yourself, however, you'll get more out of it."

I sighed and looked down at my hands.

"I hear you've been going out with the elders quite a bit."

"Yeah. I'm going with them to visit Auntie Belle—I mean, Belle Mudd—almost every week." I didn't tell him I'd seen Dani there.

"How do you feel like that's going?"

"Auntie Belle is really interested in the Church. But she's bedridden and can't attend. Her great-niece Rhanda isn't too thrilled about our visits, but she lets us in because she knows it means so much to Auntie Belle."

"The elders think Auntie Belle wants to get baptized."

"I think so too," I said. "She may be in her nineties and confined to her bed, but her mind is clear. I know she's forgetful at times, but she comprehends what the elders are teaching."

"How do you feel about missionary work since you've been going out with the elders?"

I figured this was as good a time as any to tell President Carter that I wasn't going on a mission. But I had to do it in the right way. "It's been a good experience to talk to Auntie Belle. I really care about her. I'm not an expert at sharing the gospel, so I'm glad I have this chance to go and watch the missionaries teach. I'm not going to be able to serve a mission, so helping out around here is the next best thing."

President Carter raised one eyebrow. "And why aren't you going to be able to serve a mission?"

"I got a full ride to Nelson-Barrett U."

President Carter smiled. "That's very impressive. Congratulations."

"Thanks."

"I guess we'd better conclude this interview." President Carter looked at his watch. "If you don't mind, keep visiting Auntie Belle with the elders. They need your help."

I stood up, relieved that the interview was over. "I will."

President Carter walked to the door. He put his hand on the knob, but hesitated before he turned it. "Kevin, I know this scholarship is important to you. It would be to anybody. But before you make a final decision, I challenge you to pray about it. Alone. Go somewhere by your-self. Ask the Lord what His plan is for you. I know you're thinking this scholarship is a stroke of good fortune. And it is. But sometimes even good fortune can be a temptation. If you feel the least bit uncertain about your decision, go to the Lord and ask. Will you do that?"

"Yes."

President Carter opened the door. "Thanks for talking with me." He shook my hand.

"Anytime," I said.

That afternoon, I went with the elders to see Auntie Belle.

Rhanda opened the door and let us in, but she didn't speak. She walked back to the TV room, flopped down on the sofa, picked up the remote, and cranked up the volume.

I followed the elders to Auntie Belle's room.

"Hello, boys. Hello, sweetie." Auntie Belle reached for my hand as usual. "I'm ready for my lesson." Then she lowered her voice. "First, though, I want to talk to you about baptism."

"We're listening," Elder McDonnell said.

"There's no way I can come to church. But I want to get baptized."

The elders exchanged glances. "You've prayed about this?"

"I know it's the right thing to do." She motioned for us to come closer. "But I don't know how Rhanda will react."

"We'll discuss this with our mission president," Elder Tolino said.

Auntie Belle beamed. "All my life I've wondered what the Lord wanted from me. There were times when He tried to tell me, but I didn't listen. He had to wait until I was an old woman confined to her bed until I'd open my ears and my heart. But I've heard His voice, and now I know. I can't wait to be clean."

Elder McDonnell said a prayer, and Elder Tolino gave a short lesson. I was impressed with Auntie Belle's answers to their questions. She knew the Book of Mormon better than I did, and I'd just read it from cover to cover.

After the lesson we played Yahtzee, and Auntie Belle won.

"We have another appointment, Auntie. We have to go," Elder McDonnell explained, standing up. "We'll talk to our mission president. When we visit next week we'll let you know what he says."

Auntie Belle pointed to the tissue box. I handed it to her. She took one out and dabbed her eyes. "I can't tell you how much I enjoy your visits. Thank you for teaching me the gospel." She looked longingly out the doorway to the TV room where Rhanda was sitting. "I wish my great-niece would open her heart to it. She's a good girl. She's had some tough times in her life. She wants everyone to think her heart's a stone. But it's not. It's tender and loving. I see that when she helps me do things I can't do for myself. She's good." Auntie Belle sniffed. "But the gospel would make her better."

"We'll pray for her," Elder McDonnell offered.

"Of course we'll pray for her," Elder Tolino added.

Auntie Belle's eyes searched mine. "Will you pray for her, Kevin?"

I didn't like Rhanda. I didn't want to pray for her. I would have been happy if I never saw her again.

"Will you, sweetie?" Auntie Belle pleaded. She stretched her arms out, expecting a hug.

I reciprocated. *Sweetie* echoed in my ears, and I felt as if I were hugging my grandma again. Even the scented powder she wore smelled just like Grandma's.

"I'll pray for her, Auntie Belle. I promise."

Chapter Twelve

Spring break wasn't much of a break. Several elderly Armadillians decided mid-April was the best time to pass through the veil, so we had a funeral every day that week. Not only did we need a No Vacancy sign for the Paramount, but Marcy and Marshall decided they just had to have a deck built behind their house before the first of May. So Granddad broke out the power tools, Dad and Marshall hit up the local lumber yard, and I was snared into indentured servitude. I thought it would be a relief to go back to classes at Sherman County High.

It wasn't.

Dani wasn't at seminary the first Monday after the break. She didn't come on Tuesday either.

On Wednesday, I asked Sister Hooper if she'd heard from Dani.

"Yes," she said. "She dropped out."

Everything I'd eaten for breakfast that morning churned into a sour lump in my stomach. "But the year's almost over. She's so close to graduating. Couldn't she stick it out a few more weeks?"

Sister Hooper shrugged. "I know. Her mother tried to talk her into finishing the year, but she refused. She didn't even care that they took away her driving privileges."

I searched for Dani at school, hoping to convince her to come back. Every time she saw me, she'd retreat in the opposite direction.

When I got home, I called her house.

"I'll tell her you're on the phone, but I'm not sure she'll talk to you," Sister Carter said. Then I heard her tell Dani I was calling.

Silence.

Sister Carter came back on the line. "I'm sorry, Kevin. She won't take your call."

I hung up.

The next time Dani spoke to me was the first of May, when they handed out graduation caps and gowns at school. Dani was with a group of her friends. They were laughing and trying on each other's caps. I was standing in line to get mine. The room was crowded and it was hard to get around. As she and her friends made their way to the door, she bumped into me.

"Excuse me," she said as if I were a stranger.

I picked up my cap and gown and left.

Mid-May, my parents and I drove to the stake center on a sunny Sunday afternoon for seminary graduation. President Carter was there, and he walked with me to the stand when I got my diploma for completing all four years of seminary. I know he was glad I graduated, but there was no joy in his eyes when he congratulated me—only hurt. When the stake president, President Kensington, put the diploma in my hand, I never felt so alone in my life.

A few days before high school graduation, I got a letter from Melonhead. He'd received his mission call. He was going to Greece. He wrote, "Believe it or not, my mom is excited. She wants me to get my picture taken in front of the Parthenon. So I'll leave for the MTC in June. I'll send you my address. Promise you'll write me while I'm on the other side of the world! Let me know when you get your call, too."

Why did everyone want me to promise them something? President Carter wanted me to pray about going on a mission. Auntie Belle wanted me to pray for Rhanda. Now Melonhead wanted me to promise I'd write him while he was on his mission. I was tempted to tear up the letter.

Instead, I wadded it up and threw it in the trash.

What was wrong with me? I get a letter from one of my best friends and I throw it away because he asks me to write him while he's on his mission?

Nothing was right anymore. Everything was wrong. Dani had gone off the deep end. I missed Melonhead. I was avoiding the missionaries. We had two new elders, Elder Hall and Elder Peachey, and when they called me to go with them to visit Auntie Belle—who was still waiting to be baptized—I made up excuses every time. I hadn't prayed for Rhanda. I didn't want to. And I couldn't face Auntie Belle, not after I'd promised I'd pray.

I got my box of wildlife journals out of the closet. I found the first one—the one I'd started when we moved to the Paramount. My handwriting then was shaky and childlike.

I thought I was so smart.

I took my latest journal outside. I'd started it last summer, but I hadn't even filled half of it. I sat down and began to sketch, hoping that would clear my mind. I focused on an ant. It was dragging a dead beetle back to its ant hill. The beetle was ten times bigger than the ant.

It's like he has the weight of the world on his shoulders.

But the ant looked as if he enjoyed lugging the beetle—like he was happy to be doing his job for the colony.

I slammed the notebook shut and went back in the house. If I was going to have a pity party, I was going to have it by myself. I put

Lima Bean on the couch and went in my room and shut the door.

Life was so much simpler when I was a kid.

I pulled out my old junk trunk and started going through the contents, hoping old memories would take my mind off my problems. There was the shoe box full of snakeskins I'd collected before we moved to the Paramount; at least a dozen brown envelopes full of genealogy information that Grandma had given me for safekeeping; the birth certificate for Kelsey, my older sister who died right after she was born. And a fishing worm in a plastic baggie.

I took the worm out and rolled it around in my hands. I'd forgotten about the fishing worm Herb Conrad had given me.

I leaned my head against the wall and closed my eyes. I could almost smell the flowers at Cletus McCulley's visitation. Cletus had been our first customer at the Paramount. His was the first dead body I'd ever seen. I'd been scared of dead bodies until then.

I remembered how I stood at the door and greeted the church members as they came for the visitation. I had no idea that they would become my church family.

I remembered the laughter coming from the old men sitting at the back of the funeral chapel. They were sharing some of Cletus's most famous fish stories. And I remembered the man who laughed the loudest and the most—Herb Conrad, Cletus's best fishing buddy.

When Herb Conrad gave me that worm, I thought it was the coolest thing in the world. I carried it in my pocket every day of that first tough year at the Paramount—the year I met Dani; the year I learned about Kelsey and that my parents were Mormons; the year Chuck Stiller tortured me at school.

The whole business with Chuck Stiller seemed so childish now, how I'd been so angry at him and how he wanted to beat me up all the time. I could never be angry at him again—not after what happened the day of his brother's funeral—when his dad showed up drunk, and I caught him beating Chuck to a pulp behind the hearse garage.

If I hadn't come along to help him, and if Dad hadn't showed up to help us—I shuddered. Chuck would have died. I was sure of that. And Mr. Stiller—in his drunken rage—would have turned his fists on me next. I was sure of that too.

I wondered what had happened to Chuck since then. I knew he'd gone to live with his aunt and uncle in Chicago. I never got the chance to let him know I had no hard feelings or that I understood why he acted out. My head ached with guilt as I recalled the mean things I'd said to him—and about him—in seventh grade.

I held the worm by the ends and stretched it until it was twice its original length. I had so many fond memories of weekends spent at Brother and Sister Conrad's fishing cabin. I thought about how quiet the mornings were on Morpheus Lake, how Brother Conrad and I used to fish and eat his wife's homemade fried apple pies until our stomachs couldn't hold any more.

There's something about being out on the lake, silently waiting for the fish to bite, that helps you think about things more clearly. And a special bond forms between fishing buddies. I felt that bond with Brother Conrad. He was my fishing buddy. He was my friend.

The next thing I knew, I was dialing Brother Conrad's number.

Ring. Ring. Click. "This is Herb," said the jolly voice on the other end.

"Brother Conrad, this is Kevin."

There was a long pause, then Brother Conrad chuckled. "Bass are supposed to be bitin' good this weekend. I'd sure like to do some fishin'."

This was Brother Conrad's way to invite me to go fishing. The offer was exactly what I'd hoped for. "If you could use someone to bait your hooks, I'm free."

Chapter Thirteen

Brother Conrad let me drive his big yellow truck to Morpheus Lake. He and his wife, Sister Imogene Conrad, followed behind in their sedan. It was fun to drive his truck; I felt like the king of the road, pulling a big bass boat on an even bigger trailer. My foot tingled each time I pressed the accelerator and made the diesel engine roar. The truck's ride was smooth as it maneuvered the serpentine road leading to the Conrad's cabin.

When we arrived, I helped Sister Imogene unload the groceries.

"Are you going to make your famous fried apple pies?" I asked.

"Only if you promise to eat them all." Sister Imogene lugged the cooler to the cabin and set it on the porch.

"We'll be goin' out early, so you'd better make 'em tonight," Brother Conrad said as he arranged our tackle in the bottom of the boat.

"We gotta get out there before the fish, so's they won't suspect us."

Sister Imogene wrinkled her nose at her husband. "The earlier you get out of my hair, the quicker I can get something done. Just don't catch anything you don't intend to clean, 'cause you know I won't do it." She grabbed her broom and mop bucket and made her way to the kitchen, intent on banishing the dust that had settled over the winter.

That night as I lay in bed, I listened to Brother and Sister Conrad snore. It was, in an odd way, a comforting harmony. I tucked the sheets under my chin and smiled. I tried to decide if they sounded like two moose in the backcountry or the diesel engine of Brother Conrad's truck. Right before sleep closed in around me, I chose the moose.

Brother Conrad woke me up at four thirty in the morning. Sister Imogene had been up long before that and had fixed enough food for twenty people. I ate biscuits, eggs, and country ham until I had to loosen my belt. Then Brother Conrad and I set out to catch some fish.

We loaded our gear and snacks in the boat, and I pushed us off the bank. Brother Conrad started the trolling motor, and soon we were gliding across the water. The trees surrounding the lake were green and full. The air was fresh and the sunrise swelled with the promise of a new day.

For the first time in weeks, I felt a sense of peace.

When Brother Conrad found a spot he liked, he turned off the motor. We baited our hooks and cast our lines into the water.

"Nice cast," Brother Conrad said as my artificial bait hit the water several feet away. "I taught you well."

We fished for a long time and didn't catch anything but some of Sister Imogene's fried apple pies. When daylight officially arrived, the sky overhead shimmered like a solid sheet of blue glass. A chorus of whip-poor-wills celebrated the morning with a high-pitched song. An otter took his day's first slide down a muddy bank into the water. Turtles popped their heads above the surface to see what we were up to. A harmless water snake sunbathed on a floating log.

Brother Conrad spoke. "I got you a graduation present—actually, I got you two."

"Don't you need the money for other things?"

"I've got all the money I need, and I don't need much. Just enough to keep Genie fed and to buy bait so's I can fish."

"Genie—I mean Sister Imogene—might argue with the bait part."

Brother Conrad reeled his line in and recast. His expression was serious. "Genie and I talked about your gift. When we do something, we do it together."

"That means a lot," I said.

Brother Conrad reeled his line in and set his pole on the bottom of the boat. He took off his cap and wiped his forehead. "Genie and I have four daughters—four beautiful girls—but we never had a son. Did you know one of my girls served a mission? She went to Wales."

"That's a long way from Arkansas."

"I'd always hoped Genie and I could serve a mission. But she had to take care of her mother. She had cancer. It was awful." Brother Conrad shook his head at the bad memory. "Now her father's in the nursing home. She can't leave him. You know he's almost a hundred years old?"

I thought about Rhanda and how she took care of Auntie Belle. "I think it would be hard to take care of someone like that."

"It is, but Genie never complains. She's a good woman." Brother Conrad helped himself to another pie. "Anyway, that's changing the subject. Let's get back to your gift. There's two things we want to give you. The first is this boat. When I die, I want you to have my boat."

I didn't like hearing him talk that way. "I don't want to take your boat."

"Yes you do. Besides, I've already put it in my will. You get this boat and the trailer to haul it."

I refused to let my eyes get misty. I didn't want Brother Conrad to think I was getting emotional. "You're not planning to die soon, are you?"

He laughed. "Of course not." Then he explained, "My girls don't care nothin' about fishing. I'm proud of this boat and want it to go to someone who'll take care of it. You're like the son I never had. I want you to have it."

"Why are you bringing this up?"

"Because there's two things Genie and I want to give you."

"The boat and the trailer. That's two."

"No, that's one."

I reeled my line in.

"Genie and I want to help your parents pay for your mission."

I almost dropped my pole.

"If we'd had a son, we would have paid for his mission. You're like the son I never had. I want to do that for you."

My heart felt as heavy as a two-ton boulder. I was sure my end of the boat shifted under the weight. I reeled in and laid my pole on the bottom of the boat next to Brother Conrad's.

"What's wrong, son? Your shoulders are droopin' like you've lost your best friend."

I buried my face in my hands. "I don't know."

Brother Conrad rested his hand on my shoulder. "You don't know what?"

"That's just it. I don't know."

"In other words, you're befuddled."

I nodded, but kept my head lowered; I couldn't bear to look him in the face.

"What's causing your confusion?"

"How am I supposed to know why I'm confused?"

"It's hard bein' eighteen. You're young and have a lot of decisions to make."

"I'm not ready to make them." I sat up. "And I don't like the decisions other people are making."

Brother Conrad scratched his chin. "You can't force other people to do right. You can teach them, but they have to learn by their own experiences."

"Dad said life is like the Mississippi River. If you sit on the bank, the river will eventually flood and take you downstream anyway."

Brother Conrad chuckled. "Sounds like something Arlice would say."

"Don't you get it? If that's true, then there's no escape. Your destiny is determined for you. So where's the choice in that? What about free agency? Doesn't the gospel teach us that we have free agency?"

"The way I see it," Brother Conrad said, "is that once you're in the river, you have two choices. One, you can choose to fight the current, wear yourself out, get your lungs water-logged—maybe even drown. Two, you can choose to build yourself a raft, float downstream, enjoy the view, see where the river can take you—and maybe do a little fishing while you're at it."

It was easier to feel sorry for myself than to decipher Brother Conrad's cryptic words of wisdom. "All that stuff you said makes no sense at all."

"It doesn't make sense because you don't want it to," Brother Conrad said sternly.

I picked at the frayed hole in the leg of my jeans and tried to come up with something to say that would turn the conversation around. I reached in my pocket and took out the fishing worm. "Remember this?"

Brother Conrad's eyes softened. His mouth curved into a gentle smile. "I can't believe you kept it."

"You gave it to me at Cletus McCulley's visitation."

He took the worm from my hand. "I remember that night very well." He rolled the worm around between his fingers as if it were a prized and delicate possession.

"You told some funny stories. I still remember the one you told about Cletus and the water moccasin."

"I miss Cletus. Most Christlike man I've ever known. You would have liked him."

If Brother Conrad believed it, I knew it was true. "What made him Christlike?"

Brother Conrad took a deep breath. He settled back in his seat and tugged the bill of his cap down to deflect the hot sun. "Cletus always tried to do what he thought the Lord wanted him to do. Didn't matter if it made him uncomfortable or meant he'd have to go without—if the Lord needed him, he didn't hesitate. He was an unselfish, willing servant."

I stared at my shoes. The sun beat down, burning my back through my T-shirt. My ribs ached from holding everything in, and the words were fighting their way up to my throat, like when you have to throw up and know that once it starts you won't be able to stop.

The words gushed out. "I got a full scholarship to Nelson-Barrett University."

"I know," Brother Conrad said.

"If I go on a mission, I'll lose it."

Brother Conrad held his hand out, palm open, and let the sun shine on the worm. "I'm sure you will."

"I've lost Dani too."

"*You've* lost Dani?" Brother Conrad asked as he placed the worm in my hand. "What'd you do—forget where you put her?"

I stuffed the worm back in my pocket. "No."

"Don't blame yourself for things you can't control. She knows the truth. It's her choice to stay away from church, not yours." Brother Conrad started the trolling motor, and we puttered across the lake to an alcove hidden by the drooping branches of a large willow tree.

"I know you're right," I said as Brother Conrad stopped the boat. "But I do feel like I've lost her, like she's distanced herself from me."

Brother Conrad picked up his pole again. "So now you're friendless." He removed the bait from the hook, chose a nice artificial minnow from the tackle box, and attached it to his line. He cast and the bait hit the water with a soft *kerplop*. "Sounds more like you're feelin' sorry for yourself."

I clenched my fists in frustration. "Yes—well, no. I mean, I know you're my friend. And I have my family." I shook my head and the chaotic thoughts rattled around inside. "You don't get what I'm trying to say. I wish I hadn't told you about Dad's analogy. I didn't think you'd use it against me—especially since I still can't figure it out." I picked up my pole and rebaited.

"You want my advice? Build a raft," Brother Conrad said—and then his pole jerked. He let the fish run with the bait for a second, yanked the line back, and reeled in a gorgeous large-mouth bass.

"I don't want to have this conversation any-more. Let's just forget it." I cast out close to where he caught the bass.

My attitude didn't faze Brother Conrad at all. He put the fish on the stringer and rebaited. "If we catch a few more like that one, we'll have a good supper."

"As long as you clean 'em. You know Sister Imogene won't." I forced a grin, hoping to lighten the mood.

Our conversation idled for a while after that. I didn't think that Brother Conrad was thinking about anything in particular, so I figured he wasn't upset with me. But I mulled over Dad's river analogy some more. And why would Brother Conrad say I needed to build a raft?

Brother Conrad caught two more bass, and I caught a small bluegill. We released the bluegill; he darted away from the boat and disappeared into the murky green water.

"Do you remember what happened to Saul on the road to Damascus?" Brother Conrad asked after I put my line back out.

"Yeah. We studied that in seminary. The Lord blinded him and told him to stop persecuting the Christians. A few days later he converted and his sight was restored. The Lord changed Saul's name to Paul."

"What did the Lord say to Saul when He appeared to him?"

"He told Saul to leave the Christians alone." I got a nibble on my line. I pulled back. False alarm.

"He also said, 'I am Jesus whom thou persecutest: it is hard for thee to kick against the pricks.'"

"Are you saying I'm a persecutor? I'm not persecuting anybody." I reeled in a huge clump of smelly moss. I pulled it off and dropped it back in the water.

"Your skull's as thick as Toad Suck Dam. Here." He handed me a threadbare bandanna to wipe the moss slime from my fingers. "Saul was afraid of the truth."

"I'm not afraid of the truth."

Brother Conrad started the trolling motor and pointed us toward shore. "The truth is lapping at your feet, boy. And you're scared to death of what'll happen if you let yourself get pulled into it."

Chapter Fourteen

The Sunday before high school graduation I decided it was time for me to grow up and quit hiding from the missionaries. I caught up with them after priesthood meeting.

"Are you going to see Auntie Belle this week?"

Elder Peachey's face lit up. "We're going this afternoon. Want to come? She's been asking about you."

"That would be great. When is she getting baptized?"

Elder Hall's smile faded. "She's not."

"What happened?"

"Rhanda, her great-niece, won't allow it."

"She can't do that. Auntie Belle is an adult. She can think for herself. She can decide if she wants to be baptized or not."

Elder Hall shrugged. "Rhanda is Auntie Belle's caregiver. We can't go in and take Auntie Belle out of her house and baptize her behind

Rhanda's back. That would be dishonest. We're hoping that Rhanda will soften her heart."

Elder Peachey nodded. "At least Rhanda still lets us visit."

While I waited for the missionaries to pick me up that afternoon, I sat outside by the koi pond and thought about Auntie Bell. I remembered that I'd promised to pray for her, and for Rhanda. I hadn't. In fact, I realized it had been a long time since I'd prayed about anything.

The koi were swimming around the edge of the pond, making one complete circle after another. I leaned over, elbows on my bony knees, so I could see the fish better. They circled round and round, their unblinking, zombie-like eyes bulging out from the sides of their heads.

I rested my head in my hands and closed my eyes. *Heavenly Father, I'm thankful to be able to visit Auntie Belle today. Please soften Rhanda's heart so she will let Auntie Belle get baptized.*

I opened my eyes. The fish swam as if they were on autopilot. I hoped they didn't have feelings. It would be miserable to know that no matter how hard you swam, you'd never get anywhere.

I thought of Marcy and Marshall. They'd been reading the scriptures, wondering if the church was true. I'd convinced myself there was no way I could help them; I wasn't good at teaching the gospel.

A sick feeling came over me. Why hadn't I prayed for them? If I wasn't willing to do anything else, I could have at least prayed for them.

I closed my eyes again. *Please forgive me for not praying. In Jesus' name, amen.*

The missionaries pulled up and honked the horn. I got in the backseat and we headed to Rhanda's.

"So Dani's little Mormon friend is back," Rhanda said to me when she let us in. "Auntie Belle's been wondering where you've been."

"Thanks for letting me visit her," I said.

"Just don't get her started on baptism. I won't allow it." Rhanda shuffled to the TV room. I heard the click of her cigarette lighter.

When I walked in the room, Auntie Belle reached out for me and kissed me on the cheek. "I'm so glad to see you, sweetie."

"I'm glad to see you too." I gave her a peck in return. The skin on her cheek felt thin and fragile.

"How are my boys?" she asked the elders.

"Great," said Elder Peachey.

"We're happy to be here," Elder Hall replied.

"Pull your chairs up. You know where they are." Auntie Belle motioned to the three chairs next to the wall. "I always make sure there's a chair for you, Kevin, just in case."

How many Sundays had I let my chair be empty? I was ashamed to think about it. I scooted the chair beside Auntie's bed and sat down.

Auntie Belle opened her Bible. "I have a good subject for today's discussion. I've been reading in Acts, chapter nine." She waited while the elders found the right page. I hadn't brought my scriptures, so Elder Peachey held his out so we could both see. As I looked over the verses, I tried to calm my pounding heart—Auntie Belle had chosen the story of Saul's conversion.

This is a coincidence, I struggled to reassure myself. *So what if Auntie Belle's reading the same verses Brother Conrad told me about? This is a coincidence, nothing more.*

Auntie Belle adjusted her reading glasses. "Saul went from persecuting Christians to becoming a Christian himself—not only a Christian but a great missionary. What makes someone want to be a missionary?"

Elder Peachey answered first. "I'm serving a mission because I believe in Christ. I feel like He's done so much for me that I want to give something back."

"I knew it was the right thing for me to do," Elder Hall added. "I didn't know what to expect. I didn't know how hard it would be to be a missionary. But my testimony of Christ and of the gospel has grown since I've been on my mission."

Auntie Belle turned to me. "And you, sweetie?"

"I'm not a missionary. I live in Armadillo, remember?"

Auntie Belle lowered her head and eyed me above the rim of her glasses. "I know where you live. My mind is perfectly clear. It's my body that doesn't work right."

"I didn't mean it like that."

Auntie Belle smiled and patted my hand. "You're excused."

"Know what I thought was interesting about Saul?" Elder Peachey asked. "He saw Jesus Christ, but it wasn't the vision that changed him. It was the truth that kept nagging at him and pricking his heart that led to his conversion."

"Exactly," Elder Hall added. "Visions alone don't change people's hearts. Look at Laman and Lemuel in the Book of Mormon."

"Truth is what changes us, then." Auntie Belle's eyes shined. "That's what I was trying to figure out. I didn't understand verse five—now I do. It's talking about the Spirit. Read it for me, sweetie." She motioned for me to look again at Elder Peachey's scriptures.

He handed me his quad. I found the verse: "And he said, Who art thou, Lord? And the Lord said, I am Jesus whom thou persecutest: it is hard for thee to kick against the pricks."

Auntie Belle's tone was firm and certain. "You can try to deny truth. You can try to fight against it. You can even try to avoid it. But truth never goes away. Once you know it, it tugs at your heart until you have to acknowledge it. That's what Saul discovered." She sighed and closed her scriptures. "I know the truth—and you know what? I think Rhanda does, too. She knows that once she admits to the truth, she'll have to make changes in her life—changes she's afraid of or isn't sure she's willing to make."

"Maybe someday Rhanda will stop 'kicking against the pricks' of the truth she feels," Elder Hall said.

Auntie Belle nodded. "When she gets tired, she'll find it's easier to swim with the current than against it."

My skin prickled. I wanted to believe that Auntie Belle's analogy was a coincidence. I wanted to believe that more than anything.

The burning in my chest, however, wouldn't let me.

* * *

The day after graduation, I packed a lunch, my scriptures, a notebook and pencil, and the letter I'd received from Nelson-Barrett U. I left a note on the kitchen table for my parents:

Gone for a drive. I have my cell phone. Call if you need me, but only if it's important. I'll be home before dark.

Love,
Kevin

I couldn't live with the turmoil in my mind and heart any longer. I had to be certain once and for all that accepting the scholarship was the right thing to do.

Paul confronted the truth on the road to Damascus. I couldn't go to Damascus. But there was a place I knew would work just as well.

Dad had to go to the river. That was where he found his truth. I figured if it worked for Dad, it would work for me.

I got in the truck and drove east until I could see the Mississippi. I chose the first side road that followed the river and looked like it didn't get traveled much. From there I took the first gravel road that turned toward the river. For a short time I was surrounded by trees— the canopy was so thick that it was like driving through a cave. When I came out the other side, I was face-to-face with the mighty Mississippi.

I parked the truck next to an oak tree that must have been at least a hundred and fifty years old. The trunk was so large I couldn't wrap my arms around it. I walked to the bank and climbed down to the shoreline. I searched for a spot that wasn't muddy and found a driftwood log that had parked itself onto a bed of rocks. I sat on the rocks, leaned against the log, and ate my lunch.

A coal barge chugged by, and I waved at the captain—at least I figured he was the captain. He waved back and tooted the horn. The barge created waves that lapped onto the rocks close by. One wave was so forceful that when it splashed on shore, droplets of river water hit my feet and legs.

The Mississippi was calm, and the rhythm of the current made me sleepy. I leaned my head back against the log and closed my eyes. A soft breeze blew across my face, carrying with it the fragrance of mud mingled with river water. For the first time I could remember, I realized how lucky I was to live in Armadillo, Arkansas. I was close to the Mississippi—close to a river of such history and power and importance. No matter where I went in the world, the river would still be here when I got back.

I picked up my scriptures. I didn't want to read them like I did when President Carter challenged me to read the Book of Mormon. On this day, on this riverbank, I decided I was going to read the scriptures because I wanted to know what God had to say to me.

Sister Hooper had told us in seminary that the scriptures were as much God's word to us today as they were God's words to the people in ancient times. I decided to start with the Doctrine and Covenants, since that's what we'd studied this year and some of it would still be fresh in my mind. I don't know how long I'd been reading when I got to section 19. When I got to verse 38, the words jumped off the page, and it was almost as if I could hear someone reading them aloud:

> *Pray always, and I will pour out my Spirit upon you, and great shall be your blessing— yea, even more than if you should obtain treasures of earth and corruptibleness to the extent thereof.*

Behold, canst thou read this without rejoicing and lifting up thy heart for gladness?

Or canst thou run about longer as a blind guide?

As I finished verse 40, I thought of the fish in Mom's koi pond and how they swam, never going anywhere but around and around forever. Was I running like a blind guide, never going anywhere, never thinking about where I was headed?

Was I, like the fish, swimming in circles?

I tore a page out of my notebook and folded it into a little boat. Granddad had shown me how to make paper boats when I was a kid, and I used to float them in the bathtub. I walked to the water's edge and released the boat. The college-ruled paper craft bobbed cheerfully in the waves. In no time it was several hundred feet downstream and only a small white blip in the water. Soon I couldn't tell it from the ripples that broke up the river's surface.

I sat back down and read my letter from Nelson-Barrett U. I still hadn't contacted Dr. Wallace to let him know I was accepting the award. Why not? Was I putting it off?

I picked up my scriptures and read the last verse of section 19:

Or canst thou be humble and meek, and conduct thyself wisely before me? Yea, come unto me thy Savior.

I had never been good at being humble. That was no one's fault but my own.

The best way to get humble is to pray, so I got on my knees. I prayed for Dani. I prayed for Auntie Belle. I prayed for Rhanda Mudd. Then I took a deep breath and prayed for Hunter Rockwell. I prayed for Marcy and Marshall. I prayed for my parents and for Granddad. I prayed for Melonhead.

I said amen and sat back down. But something wasn't right. I'd prayed for everyone I could think of, but still, something wasn't right.

I got on my knees again. This time, I asked God to forgive me and help me repent of my sins.

I finished the prayer, but as soon as I did, I felt guilty because I'd only asked for forgiveness in a generic way. I hadn't asked to be forgiven for anything in particular.

I turned to Enos in the Book of Mormon and read how he'd prayed in the wilderness and God had forgiven him. But the more I tried to concentrate on Enos, the more another scripture kept interrupting my thoughts.

Canst thou run about longer as a blind guide?

I looked up at the sky. "Heavenly Father," I said out loud. "I don't understand."

Frustrated, I put the scriptures down and walked back to the water. I took off my shoes and socks and stood at the edge of the river. The water was cold, and my toes sunk into the mud.

"The truth is lapping at your feet, boy," I heard Brother Conrad say. I turned, but there was no one behind me. No one there but me and my scriptures and the Mississippi.

The truth was lapping at my feet . . .

"And you're scared to death of getting sucked into it." Brother Conrad's words sunk deep. He knew the truth—the truth I didn't want to admit. I knew the Lord wanted me to serve a mission. I knew it the day that Dr. Wallace and Cassiopeia got married. I knew it when I said good-bye to Melonhead. I knew it when I got the letter from Nelson-Barrett U. I knew it when President Carter asked me about it.

For months, I'd been doing my best to deny it, to run from it, thinking that it was just my imagination, trying to convince myself that the pains in my heart would go away.

A feeling of warmth washed over me. An incredible light flooded my mind, and for a second it was as if I was blind to the world.

At last, I understood what the Lord meant when He told Saul it was hard to kick against the pricks. When Saul understood, his heart changed. He became Paul. He became a missionary.

I knelt down. My knees were in the water, but I didn't care. I didn't want to be a blind guide anymore. The truth had flooded into my heart, and it was time for me to build my raft and let the Lord's current take me where I—where *He*—needed me to go.

Heavenly Father, if Thou wouldst have me serve a mission, give me the courage to do Thy will, and not my own.

And when I stopped kicking against the pricks, I knew. And when I knew, I cried. Not out of disappointment, but relief.

It was almost dark when I got home. Marshall was in the garage cleaning the interior of the hearse. He was in the backseat, his back side facing me. I gave him a shove, and he toppled over into the car floor.

"What the heck are you doing?" he yelled. He turned off the handheld vacuum and climbed out. He was mad and about to let me have it, then he saw my muddy clothes. "Where have you been?" Then he saw my tears. "What are you crying about? Oh no—has someone died?"

I held up my scriptures. "I'm going on a mission."

Marshall put down the vacuum. His face brightened. "Wow." His tone was reverent and respectful. "A mission."

Granddad came out of the utility room carrying his circular saw. "Kevin, what's wrong?"

"I've made an important decision. You want to know what it is?"

"Let me guess. You've joined the Army."

I laughed. "Close. I'm going on a mission!"

Granddad's jaw dropped. "Are you serious?"

"I've never been more serious about anything in my whole life."

Granddad looked at me with an admiration I'd never seen in him before. "Let me know what I can do to help you. Whatever it takes." We embraced.

"Where are Mom and Dad?"

Marshall wiped his eyes. "They're getting ready for the Hadlock visitation."

I checked the time. The viewing was still a couple of hours away.

I ran across the parking lot and past the koi pond. I still felt sorry for the fish, but I knew I didn't have to swim in circles anymore. I darted through the guest kitchen. I was hungry, but the smell of the food brought in for the Hadlock family didn't slow me down.

"Mom? Dad?"

"In here, son," Dad called from the chapel.

Mom was arranging flowers around the casket. Dad sat on the front pew, papers spread out in front of him.

Mom saw me first. "Kevin! Are you hurt?"

"Is there something wrong with the truck? Did you have a wreck?" Dad asked as he followed Mom to the chapel doors.

"No, Dad. The truck's fine. And I'm not hurt."

"Where have you been, then?" Dad eyed me curiously. "You've graduated from high school, but that doesn't mean you can run off without telling us."

"Didn't you see my note?"

"I saw your note. But it didn't tell us where you were. At least you were thoughtful enough to take your cell phone."

I held on to the back of a pew to brace myself. "I have something to tell you."

"Go ahead," Mom said, trying not to show fear.

"I'm turning down the scholarship."

Mom gasped. Dad's face paled.

"I'm going to serve a mission."

Mom covered her mouth with her hands and started sobbing.

Dad pumped his fist into the air and started leaping around the room.

I put my arm around her. "Don't cry, Mom. This is good news."

"I'm so relieved." She took a tissue from her pocket and blew her nose.

I put my arms around her. "I'm relieved too."

Mom dabbed her eyes. "We've been praying for you. We knew you were struggling with the decision. But we knew it was a decision you had to make. We couldn't make it for you."

"Thank you for letting me do that," I said. And I meant it.

"You're going to be a wonderful missionary, Kevin." She blew her nose again. "But I sure am going to miss you. Two years is a long time."

Dad was still whooping, hollering, and leaping.

"It is a long time. But the Lord wants me to do this. I know that now. And He'll help us. I know He will."

Chapter Fifteen

While all the other eighteen-year-olds in Armadillo, Arkansas, spent their summer getting ready for college, I spent the summer getting ready for my mission. The first thing I did was write a letter to Dr. Wallace.

Dear Dr. Wallace:

I am grateful for all you have done to help me apply to Nelson-Barrett University. However, I have decided to serve a two-year mission for The Church of Jesus Christ of Latter-day Saints and must respectfully decline the school's scholarship offer.

Thank you for your help.

Sincerely,
Kevin Kirk

*P. S. How's Melonhead (I mean Walter). I
haven't heard from him since he left for the
MTC.*

Soon after, I received a reply:

Dear Kevin Kirk,

*I am disappointed that you will not be
attending Nelson-Barrett. I was antici-
pating your arrival. However, I respect
your decision to serve a mission for your
church. I am sure you will be as thorough
in your church service as you are in your
studies.*

*When your mission service is complete, con-
tact, me and if you desire I will help you
apply for the scholarship again.*

*Best wishes,
Dr. A. L. Wallace*

*P. S. Walter's letters to his mother are highly
positive. He is in Athens and is quite busy
with his church duties. I hope you enjoy your
mission as much as Walter is enjoying his.*

For my next step, I got a job at the Cow Palace. I was still helping Mom and Dad at the Paramount, but there were a lot of things I needed to buy. And I'd need to have money saved up for my return to help me get started at college.

The manager understood when I told her I couldn't work on Sundays. I was glad. I wasn't going to miss any more Sundays with Auntie Belle. The chair she saved for me wasn't going to go empty again until it was time for me to go to the MTC.

When I was ready to fill out my missionary application, I had an interview with President Carter. It was the final Sunday our branch met in the old Fix-Rite Hardware store. After the interview, I asked about Dani.

"She won't listen to me or her mother. She's leaving for the University of Tennessee soon. Maybe when she's at college, she'll choose to get involved in church again."

"I've been praying for her," I said.

"I have to hope she still has a testimony, that it's just buried right now as she tries to get her life sorted out. At least she's not running around with Hunter anymore."

"She's not?"

"Hunter left town after graduation. He went to live with some relatives. He's going to go to

Southern Arkansas and play football for the Muleriders. Dani had this crazy idea of going to Southern A too, but fortunately we were able to talk her out of it. I knew the reason she wanted to go there—she wanted to follow Hunter."

On our first Sunday in the new Armadillo, Arkansas, chapel, I missed the talking doors of the old Fix-Rite Hardware store. Dylan and Derek, Dani's little brothers, did too. They sat on the new couch in the foyer and every time someone opened the door, they said, "Welcome to Fix-Rite."

The entire stake presidency was there, and our regional General Authority gave the dedicatory prayer. After priesthood meeting, the Relief Society hosted a potluck lunch in our new cultural hall. Sister Imogene was commander-in-chief of the kitchen. She ruled with a dishtowel in one hand and a ladle in the other. She ordered the sisters to load me up with trays of freshly toasted brown-and-serve dinner rolls, then gave me instructions to place them on the tables.

After Brother Conrad blessed the food, I filled a plate and sat down beside the mission-aries. Elders Peachey and Hall had been trans-ferred and our new elders—Elder Tibbs and Elder Rogers—already had two baptisms scheduled.

"Looks like you guys will get to be the first to use our new font," I said as I smeared some butter on my roll.

"The groundwork was laid by the missionaries before us," Elder Tibbs said. He poured himself another glass of water from the pitcher on the table. "We're teaching families that Elders Boaz and Tolino taught when they were here last year."

Elder Rogers scooted his empty dinner plate to the center of the table and reached for his dessert plate. "Your dad gave us a referral today—Marshall and Marcy Cartwright."

"They live across the street. They're part of our family."

Elder Rogers nodded. "Brother Kirk says Marshall's been asking questions about your decision to serve a mission. Your dad thought it would be good for him to meet some real missionaries." Then Elder Rogers took a big bite of chocolate pie.

Elder Tibbs wiped his mouth with his napkin. "We have an appointment with them Thursday night. Can you come?"

"I'm working at the Cow Palace that night."

"If they let us come back, we'll schedule it so you can be there," Elder Tibbs said.

I finished off my potato salad. "You guys want me to drive to Auntie Belle's this week?"

The elders looked at each other.

"What's the problem?"

Elder Rogers frowned.

Elder Tibbs tossed his napkin on the table. "Rhanda called this morning. Said her aunt was sick and for us not to visit."

"What's wrong with her?"

"Don't know," Elder Rogers replied. "We're going to call tomorrow and see if she's better."

I tried to eat the rest of my macaroni and cheese, but I couldn't.

"I'll see you guys later." I gathered my paper plates. "I'm going to check on Auntie Belle."

I made sure Mom had a ride home, then I left for Rhanda's.

Rhanda opened the door and looked around—I assumed she was checking to make sure the missionaries weren't there.

"How's Auntie Belle?"

Rhanda stepped aside and motioned me in. "She's not doing well today. She hasn't eaten since Monday. And she keeps talking to Thomas."

I was so worried about Auntie Belle that it didn't even register that Rhanda was being cordial. "Who's Thomas?"

"My great-uncle," Rhanda said as we walked to Auntie Belle's room. We stood in the doorway and watched her sleep. "She keeps telling him she can't go. She has to wait for the visitor."

"Some people, when they're close to dying, see the loved ones who've died before them."

Rhanda looked troubled. "Maybe she's just hallucinating."

"I don't think so. God loves us too much to let us die alone."

"I don't understand," Rhanda said.

"There's more to life than what we see." That was what Brother Conrad had said to me once when I talked to him about Cletus McCulley's death.

"My Auntie's going to heaven," Rhanda said firmly. "Do you believe in heaven?"

"There's more to death than just 'going to heaven.' Maybe someday you'll let me tell you about it."

Auntie Belle gasped. "Sweetie, is that you?"

Rhanda smiled. It was the first time she'd ever smiled at me. "See what she wants."

I took Auntie Belle's hand in mine.

"I was hoping to introduce you," Auntie said to the middle of the room. "This is Kevin, my visitor. He's a good boy."

"Hi Thomas." I grinned and waved my other hand. "Nice to meet you." I aimed my salutations at the three chairs against the wall—the ones that the missionaries and I occupied while we taught Auntie Belle the gospel. I hoped I was aiming in the right direction.

Auntie Belle's hand relaxed. I let her arm rest on the bed.

I heard a sniff behind me. Rhanda was still there. "I don't think Auntie's going to live much longer."

A painful lump swelled up in my throat.

Rhanda's lip trembled. "Your visits mean the world to her."

We watched Auntie Belle's chest slightly rise and fall with each breath.

Rhanda choked back a sob. "I—I've been listening in on your conversations."

I started to say something, but I held back. I sensed the time wasn't right.

"When I think of all the times you and the other missionaries came here and how badly I treated you—well, I know you care about Auntie Belle. If you didn't, you wouldn't have put up with my rudeness."

I put my hand in my pocket. The fishing worm Herb Conrad had given me all those years ago was in there. "You didn't know any more about us than we knew about you. But I've always admired you for taking care of Auntie Belle."

"It hasn't been easy." Rhanda gazed lovingly at Auntie Belle. "But I'm glad I've had this time with her."

Auntie Belle was admitted to the hospital the following day. Three weeks later, on a crisp September morning, Thomas finally convinced Auntie Belle it was time to go.

* * *

The day after Auntie Belle passed away, my mission call arrived in the mail.

Marcy wanted to have a family dinner so we could all be together when I opened the envelope. Granddad's new hobby was barbecue, so he smoked some chickens in his new smoker and roasted a couple of Boston Butts on his new, state-of-the-art grill. It had all sorts of electronic gauges and LED displays. It looked more like a part of a space shuttle than an outdoor cooking device.

It was a warm autumn afternoon, so we ate outside on the deck Dad and Granddad had helped Marshall build back in the spring. Lily B insisted I bring Lima Bean over even though he was an indoor cat. He napped on the kitchen floor, soaking in the sun's rays as they filtered through the glass door.

Desmond sat in Lily B's old high chair and smeared his chicken and rice baby food all over the tray. When Lily B tried to get him to eat a bite, he smeared it on her face.

Lily B licked at the glob of baby food. "Dis is yucky. Sauce will make it better." She poured Granddad's special recipe sauce onto the tray. Desmond squealed with joy and slapped the puddle with his pudgy hands.

Marshall took the bowl of sauce away from Lily B. "Don't encourage Des to make messes."

"I'm helping him eat."

"You're helping him be a little stinker," Marcy said. She wiped Lily B's hands with a wet dishtowel. "One little stinker in this house is enough."

Lily B nodded, her braids bobbing. "Dat's me, idn't it?"

"I was talking about your daddy."

Lily B laughed. "Daddy's a stinker!"

Granddad set a platter of smoked chickens on the table. "We're outside. Why not just hose 'er down?"

Lily B bounced in her seat. "Yeah, Mommy, let Gam-pa spray me!"

Mom came out from the kitchen carrying a pitcher of lemonade. "Now Granddad, look at what you've started." She set the pitcher on the table. "Are Marshall and Arlice back yet?"

Granddad shook his head. "They said they'd be here as soon as they're done with Ms. Mudd."

Marcy gave up trying to clean Desmond's hands and let him play in the barbecue sauce. "I'm surprised Rhanda wants to have her great-aunt's funeral at the Paramount. She's been so vocal in her opinions about Mormons—and she knows y'all are members."

Dinner was ready when Dad and Marshall arrived. Dad blessed the meal, and everyone dove in. Everyone, that is, but me. The large white envelope from Church headquarters was on a small table by the door. I couldn't take my eyes off of it. My fate for the next two years was sealed inside. I wanted to open it, but I didn't. I wanted to know where the Lord was sending me, but then again, I didn't.

"This is supposed to be your celebration." Granddad pointed to my plate. "Those chickens died so you could have nourishment. Eat 'em."

I bit into a leg. The meat melted in my mouth. "Mmm. This is good, Granddad."

"I'm thinking about entering the big barbecue cookoff in Memphis next spring. I'll need a catchy name for my smoker, though. James T. Kirk's Barbecue sounds too generic."

"Also sounds too much like *Star Trek*," Marcy said to me with a wink. "Might as well call it Enterprise Barbecue."

Lily B gestured, trying to get Granddad's attention.

"Roasted Pig by Pop?" Dad dumped a mountain of shredded pork on his plate.

Granddad wrinkled his nose. "Nah."

"Ask me! Ask me!" Lily B cried.

"Pick o' the Pig?" Marshall suggested.

Granddad puckered up as if he'd eaten a lemon wedge. "I appreciate your input, but—"

Lily B jumped out of her chair and ran to Granddad. She tugged on his sleeve.

"What?"

Lily B crooked her finger and motioned for Granddad to come closer. He leaned over. She cupped her hands around his ear and whispered something. Granddad's grin was as wide as the Mississippi. He scooped Lily B up and set her in his lap.

"Miss B is the winner!" Granddad exclaimed. "She's come up with the perfect name for my business. Grandpa's Best Barbecue!"

Mom clapped her hands. "Very nice, Lily. Nana's proud of you!"

Lily B applauded herself. "I knew Gam-pa would like it."

I applauded, but inside I felt sad. I wouldn't be around to see Granddad go to the barbecue cookoff. I'd be out in the mission field.

I got up from the table. "Anyone want dessert?"

"Sure," Marshall said. "Bring me some of that Mystery Surprise."

Mom's Mystery Surprise was a family joke. The dessert had a crushed-pretzel crust, a layer of whipped cream, sugar, and cream cheese beaten together, and a topping with crushed strawberries in gelatin. It was one of Mom's rare successes in the kitchen—a mystery as to where the recipe came from, and a surprise that she could actually make something that tasted so good.

I dipped some out on a plate. Mom's Mystery Surprise would make a good story to tell while on my mission.

"So, Elder Kirk, tell us about yourself," I imagined a future investigator saying.

"Well," I'd reply, "My parents are morticians, and the only thing my mom cooks that tastes good is this stuff called Mystery Surprise."

Wham! The imaginary door of the imaginary investigator slammed in my face.

Actually, it was Lily B who'd slammed the door. She'd gone inside to get Lima Bean, and now she was back at the door, trying to drag Lima Bean out on the deck by his front legs. He dug in with his back claws and held on.

"Yeoooowww," he protested.

"You don't hafta be lonely anymore," Lily B cooed as she tugged. "You can come to our fam-ly dinner."

Dad pried Lima Bean's legs from Lily B's grip. "Lima Bean doesn't need to come to the family dinner. He's happy in the house."

Marshall sat down with his plate of Mystery Surprise. "Rhanda Mudd spoke very highly of you," he said to me.

"When are Auntie Belle's services?"

"There won't be a visitation, just a short memorial." Marshall took a big bite of Mystery Surprise and smiled his approval.

Dad brushed the cat hair from his hands and came back to the table. "Auntie Belle had outlived most of her family and all of her friends."

"What about Rhanda's cousin, Hunter Rockwell?"

Marshall swallowed his mouthful of Mystery Surprise and readied himself for another. "She never mentioned anyone named Hunter. She just said that the only family planning to attend the memorial was her cousin Georgette in Alma."

We ate all the Mystery Surprise, then every-one pitched in for the cleanup. When the last dish was loaded in the dishwasher and the last of the leftover barbecue was in the refrigerator, we congregated in the den. Dad came in last with my envelope.

He stood in front of the fireplace and held it up. "We will never forget this evening and its importance to our family," he began. "Tonight we will find out where Kevin will serve his mission."

Everyone was still. Dad bowed his head. I thought he was going to pray—then I realized he was overcome with emotion.

The sampler Mom had cross-stitched as a housewarming gift for Marcy hung over the fireplace.

> *Trust in the Lord with all thine heart, and lean not unto thine own understanding. In all thy ways acknowledge him, and he shall direct thy paths.*

Lily B was in Mom's lap, her head resting against Mom's chest. Marcy bounced Des on her knee.

Marcy's kids would be two years older when I got back. A lot of things would change in two years. I wondered how many changes there would be.

Dad handed me the envelope.

"Before you open that, Kev, Marcy and I want to say something." Marshall stood up. "While

Marcy was pregnant with Des, we decided to read the Book of Mormon. We read it together. It took us several months. We've met with the missionaries a couple of times, as you know."

Marcy balanced Des on her hip and stood next to Marshall. "We met with the missionaries again last night. We didn't want to tell you until we knew for sure—we felt like we needed to talk to them first before making our decision—"

Mom put her hands over her heart.

"We're going to attend church with you Sunday," Marshall said, "and—" he reached for Marcy's hand, "We've committed to baptism."

I dropped the envelope and ran to hug Marcy.

"Will you baptize me?" she whispered in my ear.

"You bet I will. I've been praying for you and Marshall."

Marcy brushed away her tears. "I know. I've felt your prayers."

"I wanted to be the one to teach you, but I didn't know what to say. I didn't know how to convince you."

Marcy cradled my face in her hands. "Little brother, it wasn't your place to convince me of anything. I had to pray about it and find out for myself. And if you think you didn't teach me anything, you're wrong. I learned from your example."

"It's time to open your call now." Marshall pointed to the envelope I'd dropped.

I stood in front of the fireplace, in front of my whole family, and opened the envelope.

Inside there was a letter from the Office of the First Presidency.

"This is cool," I said, and held the letter out so my family could see. "The salutation says 'Dear Elder Kirk.'"

"What does it say?" Dad asked.

I skimmed the letter, but I was so nervous I didn't comprehend what I was reading. Then I saw the words *Washington Kennewick Mission*. I didn't know I'd said them out loud until the room erupted with cheers.

Chapter Sixteen

That night in bed I stared at the ceiling and counted the tiles—twice. Lima Bean slept on my stomach. I patted his back. I'd miss having him in my bed at night.

I couldn't believe it had been over a year since Dr. Wallace and Cassiopeia married. So much had changed in that time. Dani was inactive, Melonhead was in the MTC, Marcy and Marshall were going to join the Church—little Des would celebrate his first birthday soon. And in four weeks I'd be sleeping in the Missionary Training Center in Provo. In seven weeks I'd be nineteen and spending my first night somewhere in the Washington Kennewick Mission.

I was ordained an elder the same Sunday that Marcy and Marshall got baptized. Granddad came to church that day. He got to see Dad ordain me as an elder, and he stayed for the baptism afterwards.

Elder Tibbs and Elder Rogers had filled the font, but there was still confusion about how to adjust the water temperature. I was sure I broke through a layer of ice when I stepped in. I tried to keep my teeth from chattering as I waited for Marcy.

Marcy emerged from the ladies' room, barefooted and in a white jumpsuit. She had her braids pulled back in a ponytail.

She put her foot in the water and yelped.

"Sorry," I whispered.

She descended into the font. "Don't drop me."

"I won't," I said with a grin.

I baptized her, and she hugged me when she came up out of the water.

"Love you, little brother."

"I love you too."

"You'll be a great missionary. I know you will." She wiped the water off my cheek, and waded toward my mother, who was waiting with a warm towel and open arms.

I got out of the font, and Dad and Marshall got in.

"Woo," Dad said.

"It is a bit cold," Marshall said through his clacking teeth.

After the baptism we went back to the Paramount to celebrate with cake and ice cream.

Mom and Dad invited the missionaries to come, too.

Everyone was enjoying their refreshments when Marshall pulled me aside. "I want to tell you something. Remember that day—I think you were in the eighth grade—and we were sitting in the parking lot?" He nodded in the direction of the hearse garage. "You said that you knew God had sent your family here, and that he'd led Marcy to your family. I never forgot that."

"I remember you looked at me like I was crazy when I said it."

"I didn't want to believe it. But when you said it, I knew in my heart it was right." Marshall set his empty plate on the counter. "It just took me this long to accept it."

I nodded in agreement. "I know what you mean."

"Two things I want to tell you," he continued. "First, when you're out there on your mission, remember what you said to me that day. You weren't afraid to speak what you were feeling. Don't be afraid to do that when you're teaching people."

"What's the second thing?"

Marshall shivered. "Please ask somebody how to get the water temperature right *before* you fill the font for a baptism."

* * *

Dad took me to Bigelow's Men's Store to buy suits for my mission. We combed through the racks and selected five sturdy, dark suits. Then we searched the shelves for white dress shirts, hoping they had at least ten in my size. We loaded up on ties and socks, then I chose two pairs of the best shoes they had.

Dad and I waited behind the mountain of merchandise as the clerk totaled the order.

"I have some money saved up. I can help pay for this," I said.

Dad held out his hand. "Nope."

It took the clerk almost twenty minutes to finish scanning and bagging my stuff. When she was finished, instead of saying the total out loud, she tore off the receipt and handed it to Dad. When he saw the amount, he looked sick to his stomach. But he handed his gold card to the clerk and said, "If you're going to be a missionary, you've got to wear a nice suit."

We loaded my new wardrobe in the trunk of the car and went to the Cow Palace for lunch. Dad ordered a Double Bacon Cow Pattie with cheese, through the garden, with a large Herd of Fries. I had my usual Cow Pattie with cheese and a regular Herd of Fries.

"This is the same booth we ate at the first time we came here," I said as we waited for the server to bring our food. "We'd bought suits to wear at the home, remember? Then we came here for lunch."

"I remember," Dad said. He pointed out the window. "I'll bet that's the same cow that was out in the field that day, too. I wonder what happened to her calf?"

I shrugged my shoulders. "I guess it grew up."

The server brought our Cow Patties, and we ate them in silence.

When I was finished, I pushed my plate away. "You think I'll be able to get a good hamburger in Washington?"

"I'll bet you won't get one as greasy."

We laughed.

"I'm glad we moved here," I said.

"So am I," Dad replied.

"I think the Lord led us here," I added.

Dad took a sip of his soda and scooted his glass to the end of the table. "I don't think that—I know it."

* * *

Three weeks before takeoff, Mom, Dad, and I went to the Memphis Tennessee Temple so I could receive my endowment.

Two weeks before, I took my suits to the cleaners, bought a set of luggage, and mailed in the payment for my mission bike. Mom called Church headquarters to arrange for my plane tickets to Salt Lake as well as my transportation from the airport to the Provo MTC.

The day I picked my suits up from the cleaners, the weather was unusually hot and humid for October. As I drove home, I had to dodge trash cans blown out into the road by the gusty wind.

At home, I lined the suits up on the window seat and the suitcases on my bed. I'd washed and dried all the new socks and decided to pin them together in pairs so I wouldn't have any orphans.

Lima Bean dashed into my room, jumped in a suitcase, and hunkered down. He blinked twice and meowed.

"I don't need cat hairs all over my new suits." I took him out and set him on the floor.

Lima Bean bit my ankle and looked up at me. "Yeoooowwww."

"What's wrong with you? You've got plenty of food. Do I need to scoop your litter box?"

Something hit the window. I pulled back the curtains. It was hail. The trees in the back lot were bending from the force of the wind. The hail was loud and it pecked at the glass. I pulled the curtains together.

Lima Bean was gone.

"Where are you?" My eyes scanned the room. He didn't go out—my door was shut. I checked under the bed.

He was against the wall, under the head of the bed, curled up in a tight ball.

"What's wrong, buddy?" I stroked his head. When the hail stopped, I took him over to the window. The wind wasn't blowing, and the sky was an eerie green color. "See, the storm didn't last long."

Then I heard the whine of the emergency warning sirens.

I ran to the den and turned on the TV. The phone rang. It was Marcy. "Kevin, get in the basement. Take a flashlight and your cell phone."

An angry red bar scrolled across the bottom of the TV screen: *The National Weather Service has issued a Tornado Warning for Sherman County . . .*

"Are you okay?" I asked.

"We're in the basement." Marcy's voice was shaking, and I could hear Lily B whimpering.

"You want me to come over?"

"There's not time. Stay where you are."

"Where's everyone else?"

"Marshall and Granddaddy Jim are in Gleason. It's not storming there. Momma K's at the church. She's all right. But I don't know where Daddy K is."

"I'm coming over there. I don't want you and the kids to be alone." I grabbed a flashlight from the closet and the battery-powered radio we kept for emergencies.

"No—listen, you need to get downstairs NOW. The weatherman on the radio says the tornado's heading our way."

The volume was turned down, but I could see the radar and a graphic that showed the towns in the tornado's path. The name Armadillo flashed in the same angry red as the warning at the bottom of the screen.

Then we lost power. The TV shut off and the cordless phone went dead. I turned on my flashlight. "Lima Bean! Come here, buddy." I went back in my room. Lima Bean had crawled under the bed again. I put him in a laundry basket, draped a blanket over him, and headed for the basement. I called Marcy on the cell phone.

"I'm going to the basement. I just wanted to let you know I'm okay."

"Hurry, Kevin. It's not good. The radio says it's hit the other side of Armadillo. It'll be here any minute."

"Are you sure? It's so quiet outside."

Then I lost the signal. I ran down the steps to the front hall of the funeral parlor. It was awkward carrying my cat in a basket and the radio too. I had the radio's strap around my arm, but the radio was heavy and kept banging against my leg.

The sirens stopped wailing. I uncovered Lima Bean's face. "I think the worst is over."

Lima Bean looked up at me as if to say, "I'm not feeling what you're feeling, buddy."

"I don't care what Marcy says. We're going to go check on her and the kids." I put the radio down, but decided to take Lima Bean with me. He would cheer Lily B up. She'd think it was funny to see him in a basket. I went to the front door and reached for the handle.

Then I heard a roar. It was like a train, but there were no train tracks nearby. I opened the door just in time to see a tree fly across the road.

And I saw the funnel cloud. It was coming in our direction.

I locked the door. The Paramount began to shake. Terrified, I snatched up the radio and ran to the basement. I jerked the door open, slammed it shut, and ran down the stairs two at a time. I hunkered down in a corner, clutching Lima Bean's basket. I prayed. *God, please protect me and Lima Bean.*

My heart pounded. I'd never been so afraid before. Was my family safe? I had no choice but to pray. *Please keep Marcy and her children safe.*

The house rattled and vibrated. I took Lima Bean out of his basket and squeezed him tight. I prayed harder. *Protect my mom and dad, my granddad and Marshall. Watch over our friends and our town.*

Then the shaking stopped. I loosened my grip on the cat, and he ran and hid under a cabinet.

I looked at my watch. I'd been in the basement for less than five minutes, but it felt like I'd been there for five hours.

I was scared of what I'd find when I went upstairs. I opened the basement door and stepped out slowly. Everything looked okay.

I tried to call Marcy on my cell phone, but the signal was still out. I opened the front door.

Marcy's house was still standing!

I went to check the outside of the Paramount. I walked all the way around the building. I didn't see any damage, not even to the hearse garage.

I went back to the front and noticed that down the road an uprooted maple tree was blocking both lanes of traffic. It must have been the tree that I saw flying through the air earlier.

The tornado probably picked it up somewhere else and dropped it here. Limbs were scattered across the lawn, and I noticed a tree behind Marcy's had been snapped in two.

Then I saw something red in the yard. I walked over and picked it up.

It was a Christmas ornament.

A few feet away, I found a toothbrush and some asphalt roofing shingles that didn't match our place or Marcy's.

Above me, a piece of vinyl siding was caught in the trees. A rag doll dangled from the tip of a branch.

An ambulance wailed in the distance.

Chapter Seventeen

I got Lima Bean and my flashlight and went to check on Marcy.

Her doors were locked. There was still no cell phone signal, so I knocked on her basement window.

She met me at the front door. "Have you been listening to the radio? It's horrible. The tornado hit the east side of Armadillo. There's a lot of damage."

"Have you heard from Mom?"

Marcy nodded. "She called on the landline. She's okay, and the church building is okay. They're opening it up to the community as a shelter."

"What about Dad?"

"I haven't heard from him." Marcy's hands trembled as she lit an emergency candle. "I know he had his cell phone, but with the signal out, I can't reach him."

"Do you know where he was going?"

"I know he had to go to Wal-Mart. And he said he was going to the barbershop."

Marcy's telephone rang. It was Mom. Marcy told her I was there, and she told her to put me on.

"Are you all right?" Mom asked. Her voice was shaky.

"Everything's fine here. Do you know where Dad is?"

"No. When you see him, tell him I'm at the church. We're setting up a shelter. Several homes near here were wiped out. Oh, hold on." I could hear someone in the background asking her about water. Then she came back on the line. "Have Marcy take the kids over to the Paramount. We need someone there to answer the phone in case we get a call. Go in the guest kitchen, get all the cases of sodas and bottled water we have, and bring them to the church."

"I'll be there as soon as I can."

"Be careful out there, honey. It may be dangerous."

I helped Marcy carry the kids and their stuff across the street. When she was settled in, I loaded all the extra canned and bottled drinks we had in the back of the truck and tied a tarp over them in case it rained again.

When I headed to town, there was some debris scattered and a few limbs down—but it wasn't as bad as Mom had made it sound. I drove for quite a way, and everything looked perfectly normal, as if nothing had happened.

"Maybe there's not as much damage as we thought," I said aloud, thinking that would calm my nerves and keep me from worrying about where my father was.

Then I rounded the curve. I slammed on the brakes.

It was as if a giant tractor had mowed down the neighborhood. Houses were gone. Trees were gone. Power lines were gone. They'd been replaced by splintered wood and twisted metal. The roof of someone's garage lay in the middle of the street.

I backed the truck up and tried to think of a different route to the church. I remembered there was a road past the old Fix-Rite building. I drove through another unscathed neighborhood, then turned onto the road leading to the Fix-Rite. A large oak had been pulled up and dropped on top of a house. I drove around a pile of lumber, and when I reached the intersection, the Fix-Rite was gone. There was nothing left but the concrete foundation. The wooden partitions we'd used to divide the open floor into meeting rooms were scattered across the parking lot and in neighboring yards.

I managed to navigate the turn without running over any debris. Then I had a clean path to the new branch meetinghouse.

I pulled up to the back door and started unloading the sodas and water. Brother and Sister Conrad came out to help.

"We've got four families here who've lost their homes," Sister Imogene said.

"Is my mom okay?"

"She's shaky but she's all right." Brother Conrad carried in the bottled water two cases at a time. "She's worried about your dad. I think she'll feel better when she hears from him."

When we finished unloading the truck, I went to the cultural hall to look for Mom. She was stacking emergency hygiene kits on a table in the back.

"Mom—"

She whipped around when she heard my voice. "Oh Kevin, I'm so glad you're not hurt."

"Do you need my help?"

"Not right now. I'll need to stay here for a while and help Imogene. I may be here all night—it depends on how many people come in. You'd better get home before it gets dark. Marcy may need you. Has your father called?"

"No. Cell phones still don't work."

"Please make sure he calls me when he gets back to the Paramount." Her voice trembled.

"I want to know when he gets home. Please don't forget."

I tried to go back to the Paramount the same way I came in, but the police had already closed off the streets. It was starting to get dark, and a light drizzle was falling. After navigating the maze of closed and blocked roads, I found a way that would take me to the state road that ran in front of the Paramount. It was a roundabout route I normally wouldn't take, but with all the debris scattered everywhere, I didn't have much choice.

I drove for about three miles and encountered more mangled trees, but at least the road was still clear. Then I looked to either side and saw that the tornado had cut a swath through a wooded area but left the adjacent farm unscathed except for debris that was scattered across the field and floating in the pond next to the barn. It looked like the farmer's car had been blown into the pond. The back end of a blue sedan stuck out above the water. It had a bumper sticker on the right side.

There was a black briefcase in the middle of the road. It had popped open and was lying upside down. I figured that whoever lost it might appreciate getting it back. I parked the truck and got out to retrieve it.

I gathered the papers together, and stuffed them back inside the briefcase. One slipped from my grasp. I picked it up. It was a prepaid contract for services from the Paramount Funeral Home.

The blue sedan in the pond—

I abandoned the briefcase and ran, leaping across the culvert beside the road. The field was soggy and my feet sloshed in the standing water. As I got closer to the pond I could read the car's bumper sticker: *My other car is a hearse.*

Chapter Eighteen

Mom was curled up on the sofa in the family waiting room for the intensive care unit, trying to get some sleep. I put a blanket over her earlier, but she was still shivering.

Granddad sat across the room, pretending to read the *Memphis Commercial Appeal*.

I walked to the window and watched the Life Flight helicopter take off—the same one that had brought my father to the hospital. It disappeared into the cloudless mid-morning sky.

The sound was muted on the TV in the corner, but the images spoke volumes. The tornado that hit Sherman County was all over the cable news channels. It had torn the roof off Wal-Mart and the Piggly-Wiggly. Information was displayed in bullets on the side of the screen. One hundred homes in Sherman County destroyed. No fatalities at this time. Seven people with minor injuries treated and released at a nearby hospital. One person with serious injuries transported to a Memphis hospital.

My mother didn't need to see that. I turned the TV off.

Marcy and Marshall came in from spending a few minutes in Dad's room. The two moved to a quiet corner where Marcy felt safe enough to lean into Marshall's chest and sob quietly.

A nurse tapped me on the arm. "The doctor wants to speak to your mother. Would you have her step outside, please?"

I nudged Mom and lifted the blanket from her shoulders. "The doctor wants to see you." I took her hand and helped her to her feet.

The doctor was waiting for us in a consultation room down the hall.

"Mrs. Kirk, your husband has some severe injuries."

Mom's eyes were dull from worry and lack of sleep. "Is there hope?"

The doctor took a deep breath before he continued. "Please understand. I can't tell you everything is all right when it's not. Your husband has a long recovery ahead."

Mom swallowed so hard I could see the lump in her throat. "So you think he'll pull through? He's not going to die?"

"With his injuries, he could take a turn for the worse. But for the moment, he's holding his own."

Mom tugged at her wedding band. "What can I expect?"

The doctor flipped through his chart. "In a few days, if his condition stabilizes, he'll need more surgery. When he's well enough to be dismissed from here—which won't be for at least a month—he'll have to spend some time in a rehabilitation facility. It will probably be several months before he can come home, and when he does, he'll likely need assistance with many of his daily activities, such as walking, bathing, and using the bathroom."

That night, President Carter came to see my mother. I figured it would help Mom to talk to him privately, so I left the waiting room. I'd been sitting for a long time and needed to stretch my legs. I walked to the end of the hall and turned the corner.

"Kevin, I—"

"Dani!" I cried.

She reached out, and I let her comfort me. We clung together as if our lives depended on it.

"I'm so sorry," she whispered. "Is your dad going to be all right?"

"We're praying he will."

Dani reached up and wiped the tears from my face.

"I've missed you, Dani."

Her face flushed. "I've missed you too."

Later, I stood beside my father's bed. President Carter handed me the vial of consecrated oil. I put a drop of it on Dad's head and pronounced the first part of the anointing for the sick.

I recalled how, years before, my father had given me a healing blessing. It was the day we went to Seven Devils Swamp, and I got bit by a water moccasin.

President Carter then placed his hands on Dad's head. I added mine.

"Arlice Theobald Kirk." The thickness of President Carter's voice revealed the tender feelings he had for my father. "By the power of the holy Melchizedek priesthood, we lay our hands upon you . . ."

Chapter Nineteen

I was supposed to leave for the MTC in five days. Dad was still in the hospital in Memphis. Mom was with him; she hadn't been home since the day of the tornado. Marcy and Marshall were running the Paramount. Granddad was doing everything he could to help—from babysitting to cooking to running errands. He'd even stood in as a greeter at the last funeral.

Dad was getting better, but he was months away from being well enough to come home. I couldn't leave my family. Not now, not when they needed my help.

I took my suitcases out to the hearse garage and loaded them in the back of the S-10. I hadn't taken the price tags off yet, and I still had my receipt, so I knew I could return them to the department store and get my money back.

"Where are you off to?" Granddad was in the garage, measuring a length of a two-by-four. He was building a playhouse for Lily B. It was supposed to be a Christmas gift, but he was getting started early.

"I'm returning this stuff." I opened the driver's side door and set the sack of still-unopened white dress shirts on the seat. "I won't be needing any of it."

Granddad dropped his wood. "What do you mean, you won't be needing it? You're leaving in five days."

"No I'm not." I put two shoeboxes, each holding one new pair of shoes, on the car floor.

"Kevin, you're supposed to be going on a mission."

"I can't leave Mom. Not with Dad in the hospital."

"Kevin Andrew Kirk." Granddad dropped the wood and set down the saw. He walked over and poked my chest with his finger. "You are *not* changing your plans. I won't let you."

I slammed the truck door. "Marcy and Marshall can't handle the business by themselves."

"That's what I'm here for."

"Mom needs me to help take care of Dad."

Granddad shook his finger in my face. "Your mom needs you to go on your mission. The Lord needs you to go on your mission. And I need you to go on a mission."

"What are you saying?"

"I don't know anyone who has as much faith as you. If you don't go on this mission, why should I have faith that the things you believe in are true? How can I have faith that Arlice will get better?" Granddad wiped his forehead with a worn handkerchief. "I need you to keep your faith, Kevin. It helps me to keep mine."

I took the suitcases out of the truck and carried them back to my room. Marcy was there, waiting for me. "I saw you carrying your suitcases outside."

I put them back on my bed. "I was going to return them."

"Did you change your mind?"

I sat down beside the suitcases. "How can I leave you and Mom and everybody with Dad in such bad shape? How can I? It seems selfish."

Marcy shoved the suitcases over and sat down next to me. "Don't worry about us. We'll be fine."

"You can't run this funeral home by yourselves. Mom can't take care of Dad alone."

"Granddad's helping us."

The phone rang. Marcy went to get it.

While she was gone, Lima Bean trotted over and snaked around my legs.

Marcy came back and handed me the phone. "It's your mother. I told her what you were doing."

I put the phone to my ear. Mom didn't even say hello. "What are you thinking?" she hollered. "Now is not the time to back out of your mission."

"I don't feel right about leaving you," I insisted. "I need to take care of you and Dad."

"Kevin, I am a grown woman. I can take care of myself. I have a business. I have Marcy and Marshall, Lily and Des. I have your granddad. I have my church family. I won't be alone."

"But Mom—"

"No buts, Kevin Andrew." Mom's voice softened and her smile seemed to come through the phone lines. "Besides, I won't have you skipping out on this mission, not when it means so much to your father. He almost got a hernia from jumping around when you told him you were going."

I laughed in spite of myself. "He limped for a week."

"He'll tell you how important it is that you go the distance. Hold on . . ."

I could hear conversation in the background, then breathing.

"Kevin?" Dad's voice was weak but steady.

"Dad!" I shouted. "Oh my gosh, Dad. I'm so glad to hear your voice!"

"If you back out of your mission now, after all that money I spent on suits—"

I grinned at Marcy. "It's Dad! He's talking to me on the phone!"

Marcy ran to the kitchen and picked up the extension.

"Daddy K!"

"Hello baby," Dad said to Marcy. "I hope you're talking some sense into your brother."

"Don't worry," Marcy said. "He's leaving on that plane if we have to tie him to the seat."

* * *

Two days before my flight, I finished packing and spent the day visiting friends. I went to Herb and Imogene Conrad's first.

"Don't you worry about your mom," Sister Imogene said as she hugged me good-bye. "We'll take good care of her."

"Will you send me some of your fried apple pies?" I asked.

Sister Imogene laughed. "If UPS will deliver 'em, I'll send 'em."

Brother Conrad followed me out to my truck. "Don't be concerned about money. I'm paying for your mission."

"But—"

"I've already discussed it with President Carter. Your mother knows too. I told her."

I put my arms around Brother Conrad. "How can I ever repay you?"

"When I'm in the nursing home, you can sneak me out and take me fishing."

I went to Sister Hooper's next and thanked her for teaching me in seminary. I gave her my address card and asked her to write.

"You'll be in my prayers," she said. "Be careful and listen to the Spirit. It will let you know what you should do."

"I will," I replied.

I went to Dani's house and thanked President Carter for being a good branch president. Sister Carter hugged me and gave me an angel Moroni tie clip, plus fifty dollars in case I needed something on the way to Salt Lake.

"Would you give Dani my address?"

President Carter took the card. "I'll be sure she gets it."

Before I made my last stop, I drove around town. When I passed Armadillo Middle School I could look at the windows and see students milling around inside LS-806, my old life sciences classroom. I wondered if the new life sciences teacher was as crazy as Dr. Wallace.

There was still a lot of debris left from the tornado. The Wal-Mart and the Piggly-Wiggly were still closed and workers scrambled to repair the roofs. Armadillo had changed forever in the few short minutes that the tornado touched down. I wondered how it would look when I got back home. Would I even recognize Armadillo in two years?

I drove down Main Street, past the courthouse, past Bigelow's Men's Store, Woods Pharmacy and Ice Cream Shop, and the little antique store that Mom liked to browse in.

And there was the barbershop. My heart ached when I saw the barber pole outside, its red, white, and blue stripes spiraling toward the top. As I went by, I could see the old men gathered inside, reading their newspapers and undoubtedly grousing about the latest political scandal or sports tournament. For a second, I imagined my father was in the chair, getting what little hair he had on his head "shaped up," as he liked to say.

I sniffed back the tears and headed for 539 Palmer Ridge Road.

"Hello, Kevin." Rhanda Mudd stepped aside and welcomed me in.

"I came to say good-bye. I'm leaving for my mission."

"When will you be back?"

"I'll be gone for two years."

"That's a long time to be away from your family. How does your mom feel about that? Especially after your father's accident?"

"I was going to stay home—you know, with Dad being in the hospital—but they insist that I go. Dad says the Lord will take care of us."

"Wait a minute." Rhanda ran to Auntie Belle's old room. I could see from the doorway that she still hadn't moved Auntie's things out. When she came back, she handed me Auntie Belle's copy of the Book of Mormon. "Take this with you. I think Auntie Belle would have wanted you to have it. Don't forget her, okay?"

"I'll never forget Auntie Belle." I flipped through the pages. Auntie Belle had made notes in the margins. Her handwriting was spidery and hard to read. "This means a lot to me. Thank you, Rhanda."

Rhanda's voice was soft. "If you have time, I could use some prayers."

"I'll pray for you. I promise."

What happened next stunned me. Rhanda gave me a hug. "I'll pray for you too. Come and see me when you return. Be careful out there."

I went home and put Auntie Belle's Book of Mormon in my suitcase. I took my latest wildlife journal and put it in too—then changed my mind. I put it on my shelf and laid a pencil beside it. In two years, I'd be ready to pick it up again.

Then there was a knock at the back door.

"I couldn't let you leave without saying good-bye," Dani said. "I skipped classes and drove home. I was afraid I'd missed you."

"I'm glad you're here." I let her in and we sat down on the couch. "I'm leaving Armadillo tomorrow. I'm going to spend the day with Dad—he's still in the hospital in Memphis. I'll leave from there to go to the airport."

Dani told me about her professors and what her classes were like. She talked about the dorm and how she didn't like sharing a bathroom with an entire hall of girls. She talked about how lucky she'd been to get a quiet roommate. And she talked about how she'd made a friend on campus—an LDS friend. They'd enrolled in institute classes on campus.

"I like institute," Dani said. "There's about twenty-two students who come. We have some good discussions."

"Are you going to church?"

Dani sighed. "No. I get lazy and want to sleep in." She looked down at her hands. After a long pause, she said, "I wasn't very nice to you our senior year."

"I wasn't always nice to you, either."

Her voice quivered. "I wish I could go back and change all the things I did."

I reached out and took her small, soft hands in mine. I didn't want to know what she'd done. Yet I did want to take the hurt away from her— wanted it right then more than anything. It pained me to know that I couldn't.

Dani stood up. "I have to go."

We embraced for the last time. I stroked her silky brown hair. "Don't give up on going back to church, okay?"

Dani pulled away and smiled weakly. "We'll see how it goes."

Chapter Twenty

On my last morning at home, I woke up to the sound of a vacuum cleaner. Mom was cleaning the den. The smell of lemon-scented furniture polish wafted under my door. I groaned when I saw the time.

"It's five o'clock," I said to Lima Bean, who was snuggled up beside me. He chirruped and nuzzled his head against my hand, wanting a scratch. I obliged.

I tried to go back to sleep, but I couldn't. The packed suitcases against the wall were shouting that today was the day. I got up and shuffled to my closet-size bathroom. I showered, dressed, and made my bed. I scooped the dumplings out of Lima Bean's litter box, poured an extra measure of food in his bowl, and gave him fresh water.

"Yeoooow," Lima Bean howled with gratitude.

I leaned over and rubbed his chin. "You're welcome, buddy. Promise me you'll take care of Mom while I'm gone?"

Lima Bean whirled his tail around my legs and chirped.

Mom knocked. "Are you awake?"

I opened the door.

"We're going to the Cow Palace for breakfast. Marshall's going to let me drive his car. While I'm in the shower, load your things in the trunk."

Marshall's Honda was small, but I managed to stuff everything in. Granddad came down the stairs from his apartment.

"Are you ready for some greasy grits and gravy from the Cow Palace?"

"I'd rather have bacon and eggs."

Granddad put his arm around my shoulders. "You're not still worried about your mom, are you?"

"No. I think the Lord will take care of her. But it's hard to say good-bye."

"I know how you feel. When I was sent to Korea, it was hard to leave your grandma and the kids. I was gone almost as long as you'll be."

We walked back to the Paramount. Granddad continued his speech. "You'll never have another opportunity like this. Enjoy your mission. And don't forget—if your drill sergeant is happy, that's all you need to worry about."

"That's good advice, Granddad."

While we waited for Mom to get ready, Granddad and I watched a *Gilligan's Island* rerun on TV. Marcy, Marshall, and the kids showed up afterwards.

Mom emerged from her room, coat over her arm and keys in her hand. I could tell she'd been crying; her nose was red and her eyes were puffy.

"Time to go," she said, forcing her voice to sound cheery and bright.

"You kids ride with me," Granddad said to Marshall. "There's plenty of room in my car."

"I'll be right out," I said to Mom as she stepped out the back door.

I went in my room and shut the door. Lima Bean was asleep on my bed. I picked him up and cradled him in my arms. "Good-bye, little buddy."

Lima Bean cracked his eyes open and yawned.

I nuzzled his face and savored the feel of his silky fur against my cheek. "Be good." I put him back on the bed. I opened my wildlife journal, and at the end of my last entry I wrote, *To be continued in two years . . .*

I stood in the doorway and took one last long look at my room. I turned out the light and walked away.

At the Cow Palace I gave Lily B a quarter to put in the Gum 'n' Gems machine. She turned the knob, and a small plastic egg came out of the hatch. She twisted and twisted but couldn't open it.

"Open it, Unka Kebin," she said, and held the egg up.

I broke it open and she took out the prize inside.

"Ooooh. It's a pretty ring. Fix it for me." I put the pink rhinestone ring on her finger and adjusted the size so it would fit. Lily B held her hand out and admired her new jewelry.

"I'll bring you something special from Washington," I said. "Would you like a moose?"

Lily B nodded vigorously.

"I'll find the moose with the biggest antlers and bring him home. You can keep him in your playroom."

"Mommy, Mommy." Lily B tugged at Marcy's leg. "Unka Kebin's gonna bring me a moose!"

Marcy made a face. "If Kevin's bringing you a moose, he'd better bring a shovel so he can clean up after it."

When the server brought our food, she brought me a platter of bacon and eggs with a huge stack of pancakes and blueberry syrup on the side. "This is on the house," she said as she set the platter in front of me. "We're going to miss you around here."

We lingered over our breakfast as long as we could. But the morning was growing short, and Mom and I had a long drive ahead.

"Be careful, Elder Kirk." Marshall hugged me good-bye. "Don't worry about anything. Your granddad and I can handle things."

"I know you can. Thanks, Marshall. I love you."

"I love you too."

Granddad was unusually quiet. We embraced. "I'm proud of you, Kevin. I know Arlice is too."

"I love you, Granddad."

Granddad swallowed hard. "I love you too."

Des gave me a big, sloppy kiss. I scooped Lily B up, and she wrapped her arms around my neck. When she buried her little head on my shoulder, I almost lost it.

"I'll see you later, princess. I love you."

"I lub you too, Unka Kebin. Bring me a moose, okay?"

I laughed. "You bet."

I put Lily B down. Marcy came up to me. "Be careful, little brother. I love you." She hugged me hard and long.

"I love you too. Watch over Mom for me."

"You got it." She pulled away and wiped her cheeks. "I'll pray for you every day. Come home to us safe."

"I will."

Mom was already in the Honda. The motor was running. I waved to my family. "Love you guys." I got in the car and buckled up. Mom pulled out of the Cow Palace parking lot and I turned to face the road ahead.

We drove to the stake president's house, which was almost two hours away. He set me apart, then told me that for the next two years the only female I could hug was my mother.

We left the stake president's house and embarked on the three-hour drive to Memphis. When we arrived at the hospital, Dad was sitting up in bed, eating a Popsicle.

Mom gave him a kiss and felt his forehead.

Dad gently pushed her hand away. "I'm fine, worrywart."

"I was only checking to see if you had a fever."

Dad laughed. "I've got nurses poking, prodding, and pestering me every five minutes. If I have a fever, they'll find it."

I hugged my father. "How's it going?"

"I'm in a cast up to my navel. I have a concussion, a burn on my backside, and three broken ribs. Other than that, life's peachy. Oh," Dad turned to Mom, "the nurses are bringing an extra recliner for tonight. I told them you and Kevin were staying, and how he's leaving in the morning. They were glad to help us out."

Mom cleared the bedside table. "So, what will we play first?"

I raised my hand. "Parcheesi."

We played two games of Parcheesi. Then a nurse came in to take Dad's vitals.

She stuck a thermometer in his mouth. "Are you ready for your pain meds?"

Dad nodded.

She checked his pulse and blood pressure, then removed the thermometer. "99.7°. We'd better keep an eye on that."

Mom gave Dad a smug look. "I thought you felt warm."

The nurse returned with Dad's pain medicine. He swallowed it down.

"We have a surprise for you," the nurse said. She stuck her head out the door and motioned to someone in the hall.

Dad sniffed the air. "I smell pepperoni."

The nurse grinned. "We wanted to do something special for you tonight since your son's leaving." An orderly walked in carrying an extra-large pizza box. "One pizza with everything, plus extra mushrooms."

"And after the pizza, we have ice-cream cake." Another nurse entered bearing a box with a Dairy Queen logo. "We'll hold that for you until you're ready. We don't want it to melt!"

"I love my nurses," Dad said to Mom. "Can I bring them home with me?"

Mom giggled. "Of course. Then we'll have pizza and ice cream every day."

Later that night, after our pizza and ice-cream cake feast, we played Yahtzee, then a game of Monopoly. We ended up calling the game because I ran out of money, Mom had apartments on all her properties, and Dad was getting tired. While I put on my pajamas and brushed my teeth, the nurse came in and gave Dad some more pain medication. When I came out of the bathroom, he was asleep.

"That medicine works fast," I said.

"They give him something stronger at night," Mom replied. She pulled an envelope out of her bag. "You'll be in the MTC on your nineteenth birthday," she said. "I won't get to see you, so I thought I'd give this to you now."

I took out the card. On the outside it said, "A tisket, a tasket . . ."

On the inside it said, "one birthday closer to a casket!"

I groaned. "Where do you get these corny cards?"

Mom giggled. "I won't divulge my secret, no matter how hard you twist my arm."

"I'll see you in the morning. Four o'clock will come early."

Mom got under the covers. I threw my pillow at her. She threw hers at me.

The smell of my mother's hairspray lingered on the pillow. I breathed it in, not wanting to forget it. It would be two years before I smelled it again.

* * *

The alarm jarred me out of a deep sleep. I stumbled to the shower. Afraid I was running late, I kept one eye on my watch. Time moved at warp speed. I had to re-tie my tie three times before I got the length right.

When I finished, Mom took her shower. She finished getting ready in half her normal time. It was four thirty in the morning.

Dad was still sleeping. I nudged him. "I have to go."

He opened his eyes slowly. "Good morning."

I nudged him again. "It's time for me to leave. I have to catch my plane."

Dad took a deep breath. "That's right." He reached up and patted my cheek. "I love you, son. Don't ever forget it."

"I won't."

"Don't worry about me, you hear? The Lord is taking care of me. I know He'll take care of you too."

I wrapped my arms around his neck. "You'll be at the airport when I come home."

"You bet." Dad's arms were around me, too, but he didn't have much strength in them.

I pulled away, and Dad grasped my hand. "Have faith, son."

"I will."

I forced myself out the door and into the hall. Those first steps out of Dad's room were the hardest I'd ever had to take.

Mom was quiet on the drive to the airport. When we got inside I noticed she carried a long paper tube. "What's that for?"

"Nothing."

I got my bags weighed and tagged, and we headed for the baggage screening area. It was five fifteen.

Mom grabbed my arm and pointed to the sign above our heads: Ticketed Passengers Only Beyond This Point.

I held my mother close. "I love you, Mom."

"I love you too." She tiptoed up and kissed my cheek. "I'm so proud of you. Please be careful. Listen to the Spirit. You'll be a great missionary."

I boarded the plane and was surprised at how small it was inside. I stuffed my carry-on in the overhead compartment and took my seat by the window. An older gentleman in a business suit sat down in the seat next to me. "What's your destination?"

"Salt Lake City."

He opened his briefcase. "I'm going to Denver on business."

I put on my seat belt. "I'm going to be a missionary."

"You must be a Mormon," the man said. "My brother is a Mormon. His daughter is serving a mission. She's in Denmark."

"I'm going to Kennewick, Washington."

"Beautiful country there. Well, enjoy your flight." The man turned his attention to his papers.

My mom was still where I'd left her. She held a banner up to the window. It said, "Have Faith."

I laughed. "That's what the paper tube was for."

The man beside me grunted, not understanding.

I pointed out the window.

"Is that your mom?" he asked.

I nodded, too full of emotion to speak.

The plane rolled onto the runway, and soon we were in the air. At first the ground looked like

a crazy quilt, a hodgepodge of geometric shapes.
Then there was nothing to see other than a
thick, white blanket of clouds.

I flew from Memphis to Dallas and then got
on a larger plane that took me to Salt Lake City.
I arrived at the airport, found my luggage, and
tried to figure out where I was supposed to go
next. I decided to look for a large group of dark
suits and follow them. There had to be other
new missionaries besides me.

Twenty minutes later I was no closer to fig-
uring out where I was at or where I was supposed to go. Everything and everyone looked
the same. What if I missed the shuttle? I felt a
pang of uncertainty. I put my bags down and
searched through my pockets for my itinerary. I
found a slip of paper in my coat pocket. It was
from Mom.

It said, "Have Faith."

Then I remembered what I'd put in the right
pocket of my slacks. I took the fishing worm out
and smiled.

"Kevin? Kevin Kirk?"

I looked out over the river of people that
flowed past. I didn't see any familiar faces.

"Kevin! Is that you? Over here!"

A guy my age in a dark suit was running
toward me. He was shorter than me and had dark

blonde hair. I hoped it was the shuttle driver. But as he got closer I realized there was something familiar about him.

He grabbed my shoulders, and his small, squinty eyes searched mine. "I'd know you anywhere!" His face, dotted with freckles, was brightened by his infectious grin. He ran his hand through his short, spiky hair. "I never dreamed I'd get the chance to see you again."

"Chuck? Chuck Stiller?" My arms opened wide. "I can't believe it's you!"

"You didn't forget me!" he cried as he gave me a bear hug.

"How could I forget someone who wanted to beat me up every day?"

Chuck laughed. "I sure am glad I didn't succeed."

"How are you? The last I heard, you went to Chicago to live with your aunt and uncle."

"Kevin, you saved my life that day at the funeral home. I'll be grateful to you as long as I live. And after all the mean things I did to you." Chuck shuddered at the bad memories. "I've prayed many nights, hoping for your forgiveness."

"We were kids then. Of course I forgive you. You had problems. So did I. Believe me, I'm sorry for the times I got angry with you too."

Chuck smiled. "That's all in the past."

"So, are you still living in Chicago? What are you doing here in Salt Lake?"

Chuck pointed to a group of guys in dark suits. "I'm on my way to the Missionary Training Center in Provo. I'm going to be serving a two-year mission in Chile for The Church of Jesus Christ of Latter-day Saints." Then Chuck stepped back and stared at my suit. He grinned mischievously. "Why are you here, Kevin?"

"I'm looking for the shuttle that goes to the MTC."

Chuck's laughter made my luggage feel light as cotton. "Where are you going?"

"The Washington Kennewick Mission," I said proudly. "How did you end up joining the Church?"

"My aunt and uncle are members." Chuck gazed at me in amazement. "Who'd have known you and I would end up at the MTC together?"

I shrugged. "The Lord, I guess."

"Elder Stiller," one of the dark-suited guys called out. "The shuttle's here."

"C'mon, Elder Kirk." Elder Stiller helped me with my bags. Then, side by side, we left the cares of the world behind and entered into the service of God.

Epilogue

Six Years Later

The morning sun casts a bluish haze over the volcanic cliffs of the Galapagos. I am sitting less than fifteen feet away from a *Geochelone elephantopus*—a giant tortoise I call Atlas because he's carrying his shell—his whole world—on his shoulders.

Atlas's breakfast is a smorgasbord of native greens with a bit of dirt mixed in. He chews, content with what nature has provided for him. I bite into a protein bar that tastes like sawdust. I offer some to Atlas. He's not interested. I set my breakfast to the side and get the camera ready.

"Smile," I say to Atlas. "This is for the cover of *National Geographic*."

I snap several photos. The tortoise's jaws never break rhythm.

"If you don't smile, I'll tell the editor to use the blue-footed booby's picture instead."

Atlas lowers his head and takes a big bite of grass. He could care less about being famous.

"You'll be sorry." I lower the camera. "The iguana I photographed yesterday was a real show-off."

I lean back against a rock and look out over the horizon. The Pacific washes over the shoreline, leaving a light coating of sea foam as it pulls away. I set my camera aside, take my pen from my pocket, and open my notebook.

Dear Melonhead,

I got your letter and the photos. I can't believe two years have passed since I last saw you! It seems like yesterday that I was in Memphis to see my best friends marry in the temple. Congratulations on the new addition! You'll love being a father—it's the greatest thing in the world. The baby is adorable. I think he favors Dani.

My mind drifts back to the day I stood at the edge of the Mississippi River and knew I needed to get my knees wet. When I knelt in the mud and prayed, I wanted to know if God really want me to give up thousands of dollars in scholarship money to serve a mission.

The answer was yes, He did.

My mission wasn't easy. It was hard—sometimes discouraging—work. The cancelled appointments, the doors that closed in my face; the long days when it seemed no one was willing to listen, the longer nights when my heart ached for investigators who I knew had felt the Spirit but still refused to accept baptism. I could relate to how Paul felt when King Agrippa said to him, "Almost, thou persuadest me to be a Christian." Those words hadn't meant that much to me when I heard them in seminary. But during my mission, they pierced me to the core.

Atlas moves closer. There's a clump of nice juicy grass near my feet. He takes a big bite. I grab the camera.

Click click click. I smile at Atlas. "Nice," I say. "Now you're cooperating."

I put the camera down again and return to my letter.

Mom emailed and said I got a postcard from the lone person I baptized while on my mission. Her husband was an inactive member. After she got baptized he started coming to church. They are going to the temple soon. It feels good to know that I helped at least one person, that I fulfilled the purpose of my mission.

About Dad—he's working again! Granddad and Marshall remodeled the Paramount to accommodate Dad's mobility scooter. You should see him zoom around on that thing. Mom said he got a ticket last week—he rode his Rascal through the stoplight downtown.

Granddad finally graduated from mortuary school. His graduation speech rocked the house. He said he was thankful that he finished school before he died. He was always scared of becoming part of the lesson. Now he's helping out at the Paramount. He loves embalming the bodies. I'm still hoping he'll join the church someday.

After Dani and Melonhead's wedding, I had to go to Tasmania. My editor at *National Geographic* wanted me to do a feature story on funnel-web spiders. For two weeks I worked alongside a research assistant named Charlotte. The first time she caught one of the fanged spiders, my heart skipped three beats—not out of fear, but because Charlotte was so darn cute. She wore steel-toed hiking boots and an explorer's vest. She smelled like insect repellent. I wanted to ask her out, but I didn't want to get involved with a girl who wasn't a member of the Church.

One day I photographed her as she milked the spider's fangs to collect their venom. I lingered afterward to talk. She handed me a card with the Thirteen Articles of Faith on it.

"If you'd like to go to church while you're in Tasmania," she said, "I'd love to have you come to mine."

Six months later, Charlotte and I married in the Melbourne Australia Temple.

Atlas is finished with his breakfast; now he's lumbering down the hill. The sun is much higher in the sky. Heat waves rise from the rocks.

Write soon and let me know how the baby's doing. Who knows? Maybe someday your son and my daughter will get married. We can be in-laws!

Best always,
Kevin

I hear a soft whimper. I peek inside the tent. Charlotte is sitting cross-legged on the floor.

"Kelsey finally decided to wake up, huh?" Charlotte and I had named Kelsey after my sister that died before I was born.

Charlotte grins as she adjusts Kelsey's diaper. "She's getting to be a late sleeper." She finishes dressing Kelsey and hands her to me. "Her baby food's in the crate."

I spread a blanket on the ground and feed Kelsey her breakfast. She bites down on the spoon and giggles when I try to take it out of her mouth.

Charlotte kisses me good morning. "I'm going to get his measurements." She gestures to Atlas. "Will you be fine with Kelsey?"

"Sure."

Charlotte trots down the hill with her notepad and instruments. Atlas is standing on the shore. The salty Pacific laps close by. Charlotte kneels beside Atlas and examines his shell.

I give Kelsey another bite of baby food. She smiles and banana drool runs down her chin. I gaze into her eyes—eyes that are so much like Charlotte's—and am amazed to discover that eternity is greener, deeper, and brighter than I'd ever imagined.

THE END

PHOTO BY JUDY FULKS, DAWSON SPRINGS, KY

About the Author

Patricia Wiles was born in Kentucky, still lives in Kentucky, and hopes she never has to live anywhere else. She is the assistant regional advisor for the Society of Children's Book Writers and Illustrators' Midsouth (Kentucky–Tennessee) Chapter. Her first two novels in the Kevin Kirk Chronicles series, *My Mom's a Mortician* and *Funeral Home Evenings,* received awards from the Association for Mormon Letters. Patricia and her husband Tim have two daughters and a son—all of whom have left the nest. Their cat Bandit, however, is a moocher and refuses to move out and get his own place.